A CHILD'S BOOK OF
MYTHS AND
ENCHANTMENT TALES

Apollo came riding over the water in a chariot drawn by white swans

A Child's Book of
Myths and
Enchantment Tales

Illustrations by
Margaret Evans Price

CHECKERBOARD PRESS

NEW YORK

1989 Edition

*Illustrations from A CHILD'S BOOK OF MYTHS copyright © 1924, 1952 Checkerboard Press,
a division of Macmillan, Inc., and illustrations from ENCHANTMENT TALES FOR CHILDREN
copyright © 1926, 1954 Checkerboard Press, a division of Macmillan, Inc. All rights reserved.*

ISBN: 002-689412-2   Printed in U.S.A.

Library of Congress Catalog Card Number: 89-15905

0   9   8   7   6   5   4   3

THE CONTENTS

FOREWORD   7

Prometheus and the Fire of the Gods   8
Pandora's Box   12
Hercules   19
Apollo and Diana   26
Pegasus and Bellerophon   34
Jason and the Golden Fleece   43
Circe and Ulysses   55
Daedalus and Icarus   62
Pomona and Vertumnus   67
Atalanta and Hippomenes   73
Cupid and Apollo   78
Prosperpina and Pluto   84
Cupid and Psyche   96
Orpheus and Eurydice 109
Phaeton and the Chariot of the Sun 117
Arcas and Callisto 126
The Golden Touch 131
Perseus and Andromeda 140
Pygmalion and Galatea 150
Romulus and Remus 154

INDEX OF CHARACTERS 158

FOREWORD

Over 2,000 years ago, Greek and Roman grandmothers and grandfathers told magnificent stories to their grandchildren. These stories were already old, having been handed down from time before memory. Yet their grace and freshness make them as magnificent today as they were then.

Many of these stories are myths about nature, imagined out of the wonder people felt for things they could not explain. Apollo drives the sun chariot across the sky every day, except when he goes hunting and leaves the sun hidden behind clouds. Diana guides the moon across the sky, her huntress bow visible in the new slivermoon. Proserpina is captured by Pluto, thus explaining the turning of the seasons. Callisto and her son Arcas, both changed to bears, are sent into the sky as stars—the Great Bear and Little Bear constellations, and given all of heaven for their playground.

Children who today know the scientific reasons for the sun's and moon's seeming movement across our sky, who know why the seasons change and what the stars are, still can feel the wonder felt by ancient storytellers. For the world still is wondrous, no matter how clear our knowledge.

Some stories are myths touching on history and geography—Prometheus giving fire to mortals; Helle falling from the golden-fleeced ram's back at a place thereafter called Hellespont; Romulus becoming the founder of Rome.

Magic and enchantment abound in these stories. Medea's magic helps Jason tame wild animals as surely as Circe's enchantment changes Ulysses' friends into animals. Gods and goddesses give magic to mortals to help them out of all kinds of difficulties, and sometimes to put them into difficulties.

With the magic, there is truth. Brave, strong heroes such as Jason and Hercules, like today's readers, sometimes feel despair. Atalanta, a fleet-footed heroine, would be worthy of a modern Olympic medal. Cupid's arrows touch people to love, sometimes making them seem silly, but often giving them profound concern for one another, and Cupid manages to inflict even himself with love. Gods' and people's faults are shown as well as their virtues. Juno is as jealous as Epimetheus is giving. Phaeton's overreaching pride and Pandora's obsessive curiosity cause disasters; but Pygmalion and Galatea, humble in their thanks to Venus, live happily ever after.

For many good reasons, then, these classic tales live on. Most are Greek tales. A few, namely "Pomona and Vertumnus," "Romulus and Remus," "Pygmalion and Galatea," and "The Golden Touch," are of Roman origin. In this edition, these stories are reprinted from *A Child's Book of Myths*, 1924, and *Enchantment Tales for Children*, 1926, both graced with the gentle art of Margaret Evans Price. These versions of the ageless myths and enchantment tales are as clear and beautiful today as they were in the 1920s.

In the first edition, in 1924, Katharine Lee Bates wrote words still appropriate: "Do not say these stories are too beautiful to be true. They are too beautiful *not* to be true. . . . Let them persuade you that you and all about you, home and school and out-of-doors, the lives you live and the world in which you live them, are made up of beauty and marvel and splendor. . . . The only thing that does not exist is the commonplace."

THE EDITORS

To each bird and animal Epimetheus gave a gift

PROMETHEUS AND THE FIRE OF THE GODS

Prometheus and Epimetheus were Titans, who lived on the earth before men were created. The Titans were large and strong and could do many wonderful things.

Prometheus knew that the first men were soon coming to live on earth, and spent most of his time, like a great father, making things ready for their coming.

He planted the first seeds of fruit trees and of flowers. He opened up tiny springs on the sides of the mountains so that little streams might come running down and water the valleys. He watched over the animals and taught his brother, Epimetheus, how to help him.

To each bird and animal Epimetheus gave a gift that would make it more useful or more beautiful. He gave wool to the sheep, and soft fur to many small animals so that man might have clothing. He gave milk to the cow, and speed to the horse, ivory tusks to the elephant, whalebone to the whale, beautiful feathers to the ostrich, and sweet songs to the birds—all things that mankind has ever since found pleasant and useful.

Last of all he decided to have ready some especially splendid gift for man himself. Prometheus tried to think of something great and beautiful enough and at last he remembered the fire of the gods.

"If," thought he, "I could go up to the sun and light a torch, perhaps I could bring fire to earth for man to use."

So he climbed to the top of Mount Olympus, the home of the gods. Its tall peaks reached up into the sky, so steep that only a god or a Titan might ascend.

From the very highest point Prometheus stepped off among the clouds. Then, walking carefully from one fleecy island to another, he approached the chariot of the sun as it sped across the sky, driven by Apollo and drawn by the four horses of the Day.

No man could have endured the heat from the chariot as it drew near, but Prometheus was a Titan. Stretching toward the chariot a long torch, he held it tightly as it caught fire although the light blinded him and the fire burned his hands. Apollo passed on his way, never guessing that Prometheus had stolen some of the heavenly fire.

Hiding his torch as much as he could, Prometheus hurried down the mountain of the gods until he reached the earth. There he kindled a fire among the rocks and bade Epimetheus watch it, so that it might never die out.

When man was born on earth, he used the fire to warm himself, to cook his food, and to frighten away the fiercest of the animals when they prowled too near at night. He learned to use fire to bake his clay dishes so that they would hold water, and to melt gold from the rocks.

But Jupiter was angry with Prometheus for daring to steal fire from the sun, and just when man had learned to enjoy the gift of Prometheus, the god snatched it away.

He forbade Prometheus ever again to approach the sun.
For a long time Prometheus considered how he might
regain fire for man, who was now miserable indeed, for
he had no way of cooking his food or of warming himself.

Prometheus again set out for Mount Olympus, but
this time he visited Vulcan's workshop, and took some fire

Jupiter chained Prometheus to a rock on Mount Caucasus

from his forge. He hid the stolen flame in a hollow reed
so that the gods might not see it, and hurried back to earth.

Jupiter, looking down from Olympus, saw smoke again
ascending from the earth. He was so angry that he
dropped his thunderbolts, raged down from the mountain,
and ordered Prometheus to put out the fires.

Prometheus refused. So Jupiter chained him to a rock
on Mount Caucasus and tormented him in many ways.

PANDORA'S BOX

After Prometheus had been taken away and chained, Epimetheus was very lonely. Men loved him as boys love their father, and came to him for help in everything. But Epimetheus wanted some one to live with him and cheer him, because he often became sad, remembering how his brother Prometheus had been bound to the rock. Even Jupiter himself began to be sorry for Epimetheus, and decided to call the gods together in council.

There was one god who wore beautiful silver sandals with white wings growing from the heels. These sandals gave him such speed that he had only to rise into the air and take one great flying leap, and in a moment's time he would be at the other side of the sky. This god's name was Mercury; sometimes he was called the "Speedy-Comer." He was the messenger of all the others, and Jupiter now sent him to summon the gods.

Apollo left his chariot and came quickly at Jupiter's command. Vulcan, the craftsman of Olympus, laid down his anvil and his goldsmith's tools. But he came more slowly, for he was lame and could not hurry.

Venus, goddess of love and beauty, with her little son Cupid, came floating through the clouds. Juno, with her peacock, took her place at Jupiter's side. Minerva, the goddess of wisdom, came also. All the deities of Olympus ranged themselves at the right and left of

Jupiter's throne **to** consider what might be done for Epimetheus.

They decided that Epimetheus must have a companion. Mercury was sent to the earth to bring back some

This god's name was Mercury

soft clay. In a moment he returned with it. Vulcan, the artist of the gods, then took the clay in his hands and began to form a beautiful figure, while Jupiter looked on and told him just how he thought the companion

13

should be made.   Soon Vulcan had finished modeling a lovely clay form, not quite like that of man, but more delicate.

Venus, goddess of love and beauty, with her little son Cupid,
came floating through the clouds

Now Venus touched the clay figure and it became ivory white.   The waves of soft hair which Vulcan had modeled became fine gold.   Jupiter breathed on the lips and life entered the form.   Her blue eyes opened, and the gods, seeing her so lovely, came nearer and gave her beautiful gifts.

Apollo, who could play sweetly on the lyre, gave her the gift of music. Mercury gave her a gentle voice and the art of knowing how to speak. They named her Pandora, which means "All-Gifted."

Venus gave her a blue robe with rich embroidery, and Mercury led her down from Mount Olympus to be a comrade for Epimetheus on the earth. Pandora was delighted with the flowers, the birds, and the sweet fruits that grew around her. She played and laughed so much that Epimetheus grew happier, and forgot that he had ever been sad.

Now, everything would have been perfect had it not been for Pandora's curiosity. There was a chest in Epimetheus' house which he kept tied with a strong cord. When she asked if she might open the chest, he told her that Mercury had left it, that it did not belong to them, and must not be touched. But Pandora was so curious that she continued to beg and tease Epimetheus to open the chest and look inside.

"If Mercury brought it before I came," she said, "perhaps it is full of dresses and shining sandals and things for me. O Epimetheus, let me have just one look!"

But Epimetheus continued to shake his head and say "No," and Pandora pouted and grew more unhappy and curious all the time.

At last one day when Epimetheus was out, Pandora carefully untied the cord that fastened the lid, then opened the chest. With a buzz and a roar, there flew out a swarm of little, evil-looking, stinging creatures, wildly turning somersaults and leaping with gladness at being free.

They were not pleasant to look at, and Pandora was frightened as she saw them go flying out of the house. In a few moments Epimetheus came running and shouting, with all the men and boys after him, crying out and quarreling and making a dreadful noise.

"Pandora, Pandora!" cried Epimetheus. "You have let loose all the evils and troubles that were in the chest!"

Pandora wept to see Epimetheus so angry. She was sorry that she had ever touched the chest. Epimetheus did not stay to comfort her, but hurried out again and tried to stop the wailing and quarreling.

As Pandora wept and listened to the strange, dreadful sounds outside, a soft hand touched her on the shoulder. She turned quickly and saw a little silvery-white figure, no bigger than the troubles had been, but beautiful and kind looking.

"I am still with you," said the little creature. "You can never be altogether unhappy if I stay; for my name is Hope."

Very gently she flew to Pandora's wrist, and Pandora ran to the door and held her hand high, so that everyone might see. One by one the boys and men looked up and saw the little figure of Hope.

Soon the quarreling and wailing stopped, and then Epimetheus sent them back to their homes. Ever after,

With a buzz and a roar there flew out of the box a swarm of little evil-looking creatures

although all the little troubles still flew around the earth to bother them, Hope was always somewhere near to help and give them comfort.

HERCULES

When Hercules was a baby he lived in the palace of Amphitryon, king of Thebes. Although Amphitryon loved the baby dearly and provided many women to wait on him and care for him, Hercules was not his own child. He was the son of the great god Jupiter, king of the heavens.

Baby Hercules and the serpents

King Amphitryon was proud of him because he was much larger and stronger than other babies, but Juno, who was the wife of Jupiter and queen of all the goddesses, hated this little son of Jupiter.

One day the goddess sent two great serpents to destroy Hercules as he lay in his cradle, but Hercules wakened as

Hercules returned carrying the body of the great beast

the serpents rustled over his linen coverlet, and, reaching out his strong little hands, he grasped them round the neck and held them tight until they were strangled. His nurses, hearing him crow, knew his nap was over, so they came in to take him up. There lay the two serpents dead in his cradle!

This was such a wonderful thing for a baby to do, that King Amphitryon boasted of it all over his kingdom. As Hercules grew older, the king searched far and wide until he found the wisest teachers to train him in all the ways in which a prince should be trained.

In one way his nurses and teachers had a hard time with Hercules. He had so terrible a temper that when he became angry everyone ran out of his reach. King Amphitryon tried in many ways to teach Hercules to control his temper, but it was no use. One day his music teacher, whose name was Linus, reproved him for carelessness and tried to punish him. Hercules at once raised his lute and struck Linus on the head. The blow was such a terrible one that Linus died.

After that Hercules was in disgrace with King Amphitryon, and the king sent him away to live among his herdsmen and the cattle.

In the mountains where the king's herds were kept, there lived a lion which kept carrying off the fattest cows. Often, too, it had killed a herdsman. Soon after Hercules came to live in the mountains, he killed this lion, and in other ways made himself so useful to the herdsmen that they grew to love him, and held him in great respect.

Hercules continued to grow larger and stronger, and at last he returned to Thebes and fought for the king against his enemies. He won many victories for King Amphitryon, who forgave him for killing Linus.

The rest of his life Hercules spent in twelve adventures that were full of danger. Among them was his fight with a terrible lion which lived in the valley of Nemea. When he failed to kill it with his club, he strangled it with his hands, and returned carrying the body of the great beast across his shoulders.

Next he killed a nine-headed water serpent called the Hydra, which lived in the country of Argos, and then he captured a boar that had long overrun the mountains of Arcadia, frightening and killing the people.

From one of his adventures he returned bringing a wonderful stag, with antlers of gold and feet of brass, which dwelt in the hills about Arcadia.

Whenever Hercules heard of a monster that preyed on the people, he at once set out to overcome it. Sometimes he was sent on these dangerous adventures by Juno, who still wished that harm might befall him, but Hercules had the help of Jupiter and each time returned victorious.

He was sent to clean the stables of King Augeas, who had a herd of three thousand oxen, whose stalls had not been cleaned in thirty years.

Hercules cleverly thought of a way to clean the filthy stables without even entering them. He dug a wide ditch from a river to the stables, and let the waters rush through the stalls into a ditch on the other side and down the hill into another river.

In a few hours the stables were clean. Then Hercules walled up the opening between the first river and the ditch so that no more water could flow through. When King Augeas came to look at his stables, much to his astonishment he found them clean and dry.

Hercules was also sent to find the golden apples which were guarded by the three daughters of Hesperus and by a great dragon which coiled itself among the trees of the garden.

Hercules knew that Atlas owned the gardens of the Hesperides, so he journeyed to the mountain of Atlas

The three daughters of Hesperus guarding the golden apples

and asked him if he would not like to rest from the weight of the sky, which he had held on his great shoulders ever since Perseus turned him into stone.

Hercules offered, with Jupiter's help, to change Atlas back into a giant, so that he might walk the earth and wade in cool streams and rest in green valleys. This he would do if Atlas would agree to go to his garden and gather some golden apples for him. Atlas was eager to be released from the burden of the sky and the stars, and promised to do anything Hercules wished if only he might once more be free.

So Hercules took the weight of the heavens on his own shoulders and Atlas stepped out, shaking his head wildly, shouting and leaping with gladness at being free

Hercules held up the heavens

once more. He went joyously across the land, splashing through cool streams and striding through the green grass.

Hercules held the heavens until Atlas finally returned with his big hands and deep pockets filled with golden apples. Atlas begged that he might carry them to Hercules' land and deliver them. But Hercules was afraid that if Atlas went he might never come back, so he asked Atlas to hold the earth until he rested his shoulders. He then set the sky again on the giant's shoulders and went back to Thebes with the golden apples.

In spite of his temper Hercules was kind, and learning that Prometheus was still chained to the rock where Jupiter had bound him, he urged his father to give him permission to break the chains which held Prometheus, and set him free. Jupiter agreed, and Prometheus, after his long punishment, was unbound.

At last, after many glorious labors, Hercules was carried to Mount Olympus in Jupiter's own chariot, and became one of the Immortals.

Apollo came riding over the water in a chariot drawn by white swans

APOLLO AND DIANA

One day, on an island in the sea of the dawn, twins, a boy and a girl, were born. Their mother, Latona, named them Apollo and Diana.

Jupiter, the ruler of the gods, was fond of beautiful children, but Juno, his wife, was hard-hearted and liked much better to pet her peacock than to fondle the dearest baby that ever lived.

Jupiter sent many blessings and gifts to Apollo and Diana and often went down to earth to visit them. This made Juno very angry.

The island on which Apollo and Diana were born was small and rocky, so, aided by Jupiter, their mother crossed the sea of the dawn to another country where there was a fair garden with fruit and wild honey and many other pleasant things for Latona and her children.

Juno, looking down from Olympus, was angry and said, "Jupiter is visiting Apollo and Diana again."

She waited until Jupiter had returned to Mount Olympus, and then hurried down to earth. Changing herself into fierce and dreadful forms, she frightened Latona so that she ran from the beautiful garden which Jupiter had found for her. Carrying the twins in her arms, she wandered far away through cold and desolate lands.

Juno followed and tormented Latona in many ways. Apollo and Diana were large and heavy to carry. But when Latona grew tired and tried to rest, Juno sent wild animals to howl horribly behind her and insects to sting her, so the poor mother, the twins pressed closely

Latona wandered far away through desolate lands

to her bosom, stumbled on, although she was ready to fall from weariness.

At last, footsore and thirsty, she came to a little pond of clear water and thought she might stop to rest and drink. On the shores of the pond a band of country people were cutting willows to make baskets. At once Juno filled their hearts with unkindness, and, throwing down their knives and willows, they shouted rudely at Latona and bade her be gone.

"Go away from our lake," they said, and threatened to harm her if she did not leave.

"But I am so thirsty," begged Latona.

"Ha, ha," cried the rustics, "then you may drink mud." And as they spoke they waded into the pond, stirring up the mud with sticks and with their feet until the cool waters of the little pond were no longer clear, but brown and dirty.

Latona stood up and, holding her head high in anger, said to the rustics, "Since you like this lake so well you shall stay here forever."

As Latona spoke, the sky grew dark, the lightning flashed, and the thunder rumbled loudly overhead. The men and boys vanished, and their empty tunics floated on the muddy waters of the pond. Here and there

The rustics waded into the pond, stirring up the mud with sticks and with their feet

above the water peeped the green head of a bullfrog. Latona in her anger had changed the rustics into frogs.

When Jupiter learned that Latona, with Apollo and Diana, had been driven from the garden, he led them to a lovely mountain on the island of Delos. There Latona dwelt happily in peace and quiet and cared for her children.

Before Apollo was ten years old he left his mother and his twin sister Diana and traveled to a fair and distant land, the home of the Hyperboreans, where spring lasted one half of the year and summer the other half.

When Apollo returned to Delos to see his mother and Diana he came riding over the water in a chariot drawn by white swans. Latona and Diana were glad to see him and were greatly interested in the chariot, which was wreathed with flowers. Apollo told them that Jupiter had given it to him so that he might return to visit them.

Jupiter saw Apollo as he unharnessed the swans from his chariot. His heart was full of pride in the beautiful boy.

"The swan chariot will do for Apollo now," said the ruler of the gods, "but when he is grown, Helios shall rest, and Apollo shall drive the chariot of the sun.

"Instead of white swans I will give him the swift horses of the day. The flowers of the Hyperboreans may wreathe his chariot now, but I will give him a chariot wreathed in fire."

Long ago, Vulcan had made the chariot of the sun and bathed it in fire from his magic forge. Ever after the chariot flamed and glowed with a light that could not be put out. Hyperion was the first one to drive this wonderful chariot, and the next was Helios, his son. Helios had driven it for so many years that now he was weary and ready to rest.

When Apollo was grown, Jupiter sent for him and showed him the golden chariot.

"You shall harness your white swans no more!" said Jupiter. "Take the sun into your keeping, and drive the chariot of the sun and the four horses of the day!"

Apollo sprang into the chariot, amazed and delighted at its wonderful beauty. Helios showed him the way he must go, and watched the sun rise in the sky and journey toward the west, glad indeed that Apollo was old enough to drive, so that he might give up his journeyings and rest.

That evening, when Apollo had returned his horses to their stables and had hidden his chariot behind banks of purple clouds, he hurried back to his mother and his sister Diana and told them of Jupiter's gift and of his journey across the heavens.

When Diana heard of the honor that had fallen to her brother, she was both proud and vexed.

"You have journeyed to the land of the Hyperboreans and visited many other places that I have not seen," she said. "While I stayed with our mother and cheered her, you rode in your swan-drawn chariot wherever you wished, and now Jupiter gives you the sun to drive and gives nothing at all to me.

"Tomorrow before dawn, when you go to Mount Olympus, I am going with you. I shall remind Jupiter

Apollo and Diana go to Mount Olympus

that I am your twin, and if you light the sky by day with the chariot of Helios, then I must have Thea's silver fire to light the heavens when you rest."

In the morning Apollo rose early to present himself to Jupiter before driving the chariot. Diana rose also and went with him to Mount Olympus.

Jupiter was much surprised to see the fair twin sister of Apollo, for he had not thought of Diana for a long time. He remembered how lovely she had been when a child, and he saw that now she was even more beautiful.

When Jupiter heard that Diana wished to light the sky at night, he gave the silver orb of the moon into her keeping.

When Apollo has finished his course and hides his lofty chariot behind the evening clouds, Diana enters her car and drives her milk-white steeds across the broad pathway of heaven. Then, while her brother sleeps, she lights the earth and sea and heavens with her soft, silvery light.

PEGASUS AND BELLEROPHON

Pegasus was a wonderful winged horse which belonged to Minerva, the gray-eyed goddess who watched over heroes and gave wisdom and skill to all those who truly wished it.

Now it happened that after Minerva had caught and tamed Pegasus, the winged horse, she did not care to ride him herself, but knew no mortal who deserved to own him. So Minerva gave Pegasus to the nymphs to care for until she could find a youth brave enough and wise enough to ride him.

The nymphs were happy caring for Pegasus. They brushed him, combed his mane, and fed him, but they knew that by and by he would belong to a mortal master who would come and ride him away.

At last in Corinth there was born a little prince named Bellerophon. Glaucus, his father, had more skill in handling horses than any other man. As Bellerophon grew up, his father trained him and taught him all he knew, so that while Bellerophon was still very young he under-stood the ways of horses and learned to ride them.

All this time the winged horse was without a master.

When Bellerophon was sixteen he began to long for travel and adventure in other lands, so he set out to visit a neighboring king.

Many friends came to bid the gallant young man good-by and wish him well, but there was one, named Proetus, who pretended to be Bellerophon's friend, but who really wished for him the worst that might happen. Proetus was jealous of Prince Bellerophon, and hoped that the young hero might not return from the journey.

While still very young, Bellerophon understood the ways of horses

It happened that Proetus was the son-in-law of Iobates, king of Lycia, and so, pretending friendship, Proetus gave Bellerophon a letter to carry to the king. Bellerophon, knowing nothing of the wicked words that were in this letter, put it carefully in the pocket of his tunic and rode gayly away.

When he reached Lycia, the home of Iobates, he found great sorrow in the land and all the people mourning. Each night a monster called the Chimaera came down the valley and carried off women and children, sheep and oxen. The mountain where he lived was white with the bones of his victims.

Bellerophon rode through the mourning city and came to the palace of the king. He presented himself to Iobates and gave him the letter.

As the king read, his face darkened and he seemed

Minerva, the gray-eyed goddess

troubled, for the letter asked that Bellerophon should be put to death. The king did not like to heed the request in this strange letter, yet he wished to please his son-in-law. He knew that to kill a guest would be a wicked deed and against the laws of kindness to a visitor, and might also bring war on him from the land where the young prince lived. So he decided to send Bellerophon to slay the Chimaera, thinking he never could come back alive.

Bellerophon was not the least bit afraid, because he longed for adventure, and his heart was filled with a great desire to overcome this dark and evil monster, free the kingdom from fear, and make the mourning people happy.

But before starting out he found the oldest and wisest man in the whole kingdom and asked his advice. This aged man was named Polyidus. When he saw that Bellerophon was young and full of courage, yet humble enough to ask help from some one older, Polyidus told him a secret which no one else in the kingdom knew.

He told him of Minerva's winged horse, which he had once seen drinking at a spring deep in the forest.

"If you sleep all night in Minerva's temple," said the old man, "and offer gifts at her altar, she may help you to find the horse."

Bellerophon went to the temple, and as he slept he dreamed that he saw Minerva, clad in silver armor, her gray eyes shining as if they held sparks of fire. Plumes of blue and rose and violet floated from her helmet She carried a golden bridle in her hand and told Bellerophon how he might reach the well where Pegasus came to drink.

When Bellerophon awakened, he saw the golden bridle on the temple floor beside him, and knew Minerva really had visited him. Then with the bridle over his arm he set out on his journey through the forest. When he found the well, he hid himself among the bushes near by to watch for the coming of the winged horse. At length

Pegasus flew wildly over the sea and the mountains

Bellerophon saw the winged horse flying far up in the sky. Nearer and nearer he wheeled until his silver feet touched the green grass beside the spring.

As Pegasus bent his head to drink, Bellerophon sprang from his hiding place and caught him by the mane. Before Pegasus knew what had happened, the golden bridle was slipped over his head, and Bellerophon had leaped to his back and was sitting between his outspread wings.

Pegasus rose into the air and darted wildly through the sky, now flying high among the clouds, now diving swiftly toward the earth. He reared and plunged, trying to shake Bellerophon from his back. He flew wildly over the sea and the mountains all the way to Africa and back. He flew over Thebes and over Corinth, and people looking up into the sky thought they saw some strange bird passing overhead.

But Bellerophon understood how to handle fierce horses, for he remembered the things his father had taught him. At last Pegasus knew he had found his master and, tired and panting, sank down to the grass beside the well.

After Pegasus had rested, Bellerophon armed himself with a long spear and rode toward the mountain where dwelt the Chimaera.

There on a ledge of rock outside his cave the monster lay basking in the sunlight. He was partly like a lion and partly like a dragon. He lay with his lion's head resting between his paws and his long green tail, like that of a lizard, curled around him.

With one strong thrust, Bellerophon sent his spear through the heart of the Chimaera

Bellerophon rode his horse as near as he dared to the ledge on which the dragon lay, then raised his spear to strike at the Chimaera, but the great beast blew out clouds of smoke and fire, and Pegasus drew back in terror.

As the monster drew in his breath for another puff, Bellerophon rode close to the ledge and with one strong thrust sent his spear through the heart of the Chimaera.

When the young prince came back to the palace, riding the winged horse and carrying the head of the dreadful Chimaera, there was wild rejoicing in Lycia. Everyone admired and praised Bellerophon, and crowded around the wonderful horse, amazed at his wings and his silver feet.

The young daughter of King Iobates, who came out on the portico of the palace to see the hero and his horse, fell in love with Bellerophon the moment she saw the young warrior sitting so proudly between the white wings of Pegasus. King Iobates led her to Bellerophon and gave her to him for his bride.

For a long time they were happy together. Bellerophon and Pegasus went on many adventures, and when Iobates died Bellerophon became king.

At last one day Bellerophon thought of a most daring adventure. He decided he would try to ride Pegasus to Mount Olympus and visit the gods.

Minerva appeared and warned him that the gods would be angry, but he mounted his horse and rose high into the clouds, urging Pegasus up toward the summit of Mount Olympus.

Jupiter looked down and, seeing the horse approaching, was angry to think that any mortal should dare approach the home of the gods. He caused a gadfly to light on Pegasus and sting his neck and his shoulders and his nose.

Pegasus was so startled by this that at once he reared wheeled among the clouds, leaping wildly in the air, and Bellerophon was thrown from his back and dropped down to earth.

Minerva, causing him to land where the ground was soft, spared his life, but as long as he lived Bellerophon wandered, crippled and lonely, seeking all over the earth for his wonderful winged horse.

But Pegasus never again returned to him.

JASON AND THE GOLDEN FLEECE

There was once a young prince named Jason. His parents ruled over Iolcus, in Thessaly. Their kingdom

Chiron the centaur

was filled with happiness and peace, for they were wise and good and noble.

But one day the King's brother, Pelias, came riding at the head of an army. He made war on Iolcus, and took the kingdom from Jason's father. Pelias had evil in his heart, and would have killed his brother and Prince Jason, but they fled and hid themselves among lowly people who loved them.

Now, there was at this time a strange and wonderful school in the mountains of Thessaly, a school where the princes of Greece were taught and made strong of body and brave of heart.

Chiron, the centaur, kept this school and reared the young princes. He taught them how to hunt and to fight and to sing, how to take care of their bodies and to bear themselves according to their birth.

So Jason, being still a little boy, was sent to this wonderful school. Here he grew up with the other Greek princes of his age.

At last came the time when Chiron told him the story of the evil King Pelias, who had stolen the kingdom of Iolcus and had driven Jason's father from his throne.

Jason was brown and strong and hardened by Chiron's training. He girded on his sword and set out to take the kingdom away from Pelias.

It was early in spring, and as he journeyed he came to a swollen stream and saw an aged woman gazing in despair at the waters she could not cross.

Jason remembered his training as a prince, and offered to carry her across. He lifted her to his back and she gave him her staff for support. He stepped into the swift-running stream, which no one else had dared cross and although he bent under the weight of his burden he fought bravely against the waters with all his strength.

At last he reached the opposite bank and set the old woman on the grass. Suddenly, in a flash of light, she was transformed into the glorious figure of Juno, queen of the gods. At her feet stood a peacock. Its purple and blue and green tail feathers swept over the grass and its shining head rested against her hand.

The goddess promised aid and protection to Jason forever after, and vanished as quickly as she had appeared. So in all his undertakings Jason was watched over and blessed by Juno in return for his kindness to her.

At last Jason reached Iolcus and demanded the throne from Pelias. That crafty and wicked old King did not refuse him at once. A banquet was prepared, and with every appearance of kindness, King Pelias did honor to young Jason. The King feasted him and seemed to welcome him to Iolcus, but in reality he planned his death.

While they ate, the bards gathered around the hall and sang of heroes and brave deeds, as bards were accustomed to sing at banquets of kings.

They sang of the story of Phrixus and Helle, the two Greek children who escaped from their wicked step-mother, riding on the back of Mercury's golden-fleeced ram. They sang of how Nephele, the real mother, weeping and heavy of heart, placed her little son and daughter on the ram's back and watched them as they sped away from Thessaly. The ram leapt into the air and flew through the clouds as if he had wings. They passed over the sea toward Colchis, the kingdom of their uncle, where they knew they would be safe.

The bards touched their lute strings sadly, and sang of how little Helle became frightened, as she looked down upon the tossing sea, and how she fell from the ram's back into the water, which ever after was called Hellespont.

But Phrixus clung fast and reached Colchis in safety. He offered the ram as a thank-offering to the gods, and hung the Golden Fleece high on an oak tree, setting a fearful dragon to guard it.

Here after all the years it still hung, waiting for some young hero to come and conquer and claim it.

The bards sang of the glory of the Fleece, of its glittering richness, and of the heroes who had died seeking it. Pelias noticed how Jason's eyes were shining. He knew that the song had moved him and rightly guessed that Jason longed to go in search of this Golden Fleece.

Pelias thought that this would be a good way to bring about Jason's death. The dragon had killed many other youths who had been rash enough to seek the Golden Fleece, and Pelias felt certain that Jason would perish also. So he leaned toward the young prince and urged him to set out on the adventure and bring back the Fleece which rightfully belonged to Thessaly.

Jason sprang from his seat and vowed that he would go.

First he visited Juno's temple and asked for help on his journey. She gave him the limb of a mighty and wonderful oak for the figurehead of his boat, which would speak to him in time of danger, and advise and warn him on his voyage.

The ram leapt into the air and flew through the clouds as if he had wings

Juno sped them on their way with favorable winds

Then Juno bade Minerva provide a swift-sailing vessel, made from the wood of pine trees which grew on Mount Pelion.

Jason called his vessel the Argo, and sent for the young princes of Chiron's school to come with him and help in the search for the Golden Fleece.

Hercules came and also Admetus, Theseus, Orpheus, Castor and Pollux, all the bravest and noblest heroes of Greece, anxious to take part in this adventure and to bring the Golden Fleece back to Thessaly.

Juno sped them on their way with favorable winds,

and the Argo sailed swiftly toward Colchis. When
danger threatened, the branch of the talking oak spoke
wise words of help and counsel. It guided them safely

Medea was skilled in all manner of enchantments and magic

between the clashing rocks of the Symplegades, and past
the land of the cruel Harpies. So they came at last,
after many adventures, to Colchis, the kingdom of Eetes.

Now the Fleece had hung for so long in his realm that
King Eetes was unwilling to part with it. Like Pelias,
he was crafty and full of wiles, and did not refuse Jason,
but agreed to give him the Fleece on certain conditions.

First Jason must catch and harness two wild, fire-breathing bulls, then plough a stony field, sacred to Mars. After that he must sow the field with dragon's teeth and conquer the host of armed men which would grow from them. Last of all, he must overcome the dragon which coiled around the foot of the oak and guarded the Fleece.

Jason feared that these tasks were impossible for any mortal to fulfil without the help of the gods. So he hurried down to the vessel to speak with the branch of the talking oak. On his way he met Medea, the princess of Colchis. She was young and beautiful and skilled in all manner of enchantments and magic. Her heart was filled with kindness toward the brave young stranger and she wished to help him.

She gave Jason her strongest charms and her wisest counsel. By the aid of Medea's magic he caught the fiery bulls as they came roaring from their pasture. He harnessed them and drove them over the stony field, and made them drag the heavy plough which turned the earth in dark furrows.

Eetes was amazed, for no one had ever yoked or harnessed these bulls before.

When the field was ready, Jason asked for the dragon's teeth, and Eetes gave them to him in a helmet. Up and down the long furrows he sowed them, and when the last one was in the ground, he ploughed the earth again, and covered them and waited.

Long rows of shining spears began to pierce the ground

Jason and the fiery bulls

and to shoot up into the air. Then rose the plumed helmets of a thousand soldiers; then their shields, and their bodies.

They stood, full armed and fierce, looking over the field. When they beheld Jason, they ran toward him with waving spears and a clatter of shields.

From his pocket Jason took a magic stone which Medea had given him. He threw it into the midst of the thousand soldiers; it fell among them like discord itself. Each soldier thought another had thrown it, and each man began to fight his neighbor. More and more furiously they fought. Soon the ploughed field was covered with fallen soldiers. They continued to kill one another until not one was left.

Then Medea led Jason to the sacred grove where the dragon watched beside the Fleece. The huge monster rose

All the soldiers stood full armed and fierce

up, roaring terribly, as Jason approached. He breathed clouds of smoke and fire and lashed his tail against the oak tree.

Jason bravely advanced until he was so near that he could feel the heat of the flames that poured from the dragon's throat. Then he took a magic liquid, which Medea had given him, and threw it straight into the face of the dragon. In a moment the monster fell back to the earth, and coiling himself lazily on the grass, went to sleep.

Jason climbed the tree and brought down the wonderful glittering Fleece, then hurried back to his ship.

The monster coiled himself lazily beneath the tree

Because she loved him, Medea left her father's land and sailed away in the Argo with Jason and his comrades. But, sad to relate, they did not live happily ever after, for Medea knew so much sorcery that she was forever practicing new magic and often she brought trouble on herself and Jason.

On the way back to Thessaly they passed through many dangers, but at last, with Juno's help, came safely home.

Jason and his comrades forced the evil King Pelias to give back the throne. Once more the people of Thessaly lived in happiness and peace under the rule of their own rightful king.

CIRCE AND ULYSSES

There was once a beautiful enchantress named Circe. Her palace stood in a grove on the island of Eaea. Here she lived alone and spent her time in studying magic.

The great Ulysses

She learned all sorts of sorcery and tricks, and became so clever that she could turn men into whatever beasts she liked.

When strangers landed on her island, she changed them into lions and wolves and pigs. Her garden was full of enchanted animals, which wandered back and forth, remembering that they were really men. They longed to speak, but could only grunt or growl. Her pig sties were crowded. But in all her palace there was no friend or servant, or any living person to keep her company.

One day a ship dropped anchor in the bay, and a band of sailors came wading ashore for water. Their leader was the great Ulysses. He was on his voyage home to Ithaca, and had been through many dangers and hardships. His men were very hungry, and their clothes were ragged and travel stained.

Ulysses climbed a hill so that he might look around him and judge if the island were a safe place for them to land. He saw no people or houses of any sort, but only a thin spiral of smoke rising from a distant grove. He hoped that this was the fire of a friendly hearth, and went back to his men and sent half of them, under a leader named Eurylochus, to explore the island. Ulysses and the rest of the crew remained to watch the boat.

Eurylochus led his men through the woods toward the smoke, and at last they saw a beautiful palace, half hidden by trees. The columns gleamed like white marble, and a fountain sprayed into the air. The men were sure they would be received with kindness in so fair a palace.

But as they came still nearer, they were terrified to see wild animals roaming through the gardens. There were lions and tigers and wolves walking sleepily back and forth among the trees. Eurylochus and his comrades drew back and hid themselves where they could watch. They noticed that the animals were drowsy and quiet. Soon the men gathered courage to steal toward the palace.

The beasts did not leap at them, or roar, but made low gentle sounds, and crowded around Eurylochus. They lay on the ground at his feet, and tried to lick his hands. He thought he saw a pleading look in their eyes. Indeed, he had never before seen such eyes in any animals. They were like the eyes of men in trouble.

He patted their heads and walked on toward the entrance of the palace, where he heard music and the sound of singing.

He called aloud, and a lovely woman, veiled in many garments, came floating toward him. Her thin scarfs fluttered in the soft wind, and her voice, as she invited the strangers to enter, was low and sweet.

They crowded into the palace, delighted at her welcome, but Eurylochus looked into her eyes and saw that they were small and cruel. He felt he would rather stay outside with the animals than follow her inside the huge door.

As the doors clanged together behind his comrades, the beasts uttered such mournful sounds that Eurylochus hid himself beside one of the windows. There he could see what happened in the palace and help his friends if they fell into danger.

He saw them seated at a great banqueting table, with warm food and fruit before them and all manner of sweet things. While they ate, the air was filled with perfume and soft music. Eurylochus was very hungry himself, and the sight of the food almost made him wish that he had entered with his companions.

When the men had finished, they stretched themselves on the stone benches to rest, or sat sleepily in their chairs. Then their hostess took a little ivory wand in her hand and touched them very lightly, one by one. At once long

Circe took an ivory wand in her hand and touched the men one by one

ears began to spring from their heads, and their bodies were covered with bristles. Hoofs took the place of their hands and feet, and they fell to the floor on all fours.

Before Eurylochus knew what was happening, his comrades had vanished, and in their stead a dozen grunting pigs waddled around the banquet hall.

Then he knew that their lovely hostess was Circe, the enchantress. He understood why the lions and tigers had looked at him so sadly, and had made such mournful sounds when the doors had closed behind his friends.

As he watched, he saw Circe lead her pigs out of the palace and shut them in a dirty sty. She threw them a bagful of acorns, and laughed at them as they crowded to the fence, looking up at her pleadingly.

Eurylochus ran back to the ship and told the others what had happened. Ulysses at once started out to rescue his men, depending only upon his sword. As he hurried through the woods, the god Mercury appeared to him.

"However brave you may be," said the god, "your sword will not overcome the magic of Circe. But if you carry this sprig of green in your hand, it will keep you safe from her sorcery."

He put a branch of a plant called Moly into the hand of Ulysses, and vanished. Still holding the green sprig, Ulysses entered the palace garden. The beasts crowded close around him and followed him to the door.

Circe herself came to meet him, much pleased to have another victim as handsome and strong as Ulysses.

She seated him at the banquet table, and smiled as she watched him eat, thinking what a fine large boar he would make. But when she touched him with her wand, the power of the little plant turned her magic aside.

Ulysses did not fall to the floor, nor waddle away grunting. Instead he drew his sword and rushed at her, commanding her to release his friends.

Circe was so frightened that she knelt before him and begged him to spare her. She promised to free all her prisoners, even the lions and wolves in the garden. She agreed to help Ulysses on his journey, and to provide food and water for him to carry away in his ship.

She ran to the pig sties and as she touched each one of the boars, it changed again into its own form.

The beasts in the garden became men, and spoke to one another once more in words instead of in growls. They thought only of returning to their own homes and friends, and began to make plans for their journey.

Circe kept her promise and helped Ulysses on his voyage. She provided him with all manner of good things, and warned him of dangers which he might meet on the sea.

Seeing that the clothes of Ulysses and his friends were travel-stained and worn, she gave them beautiful robes from her own chests. She made a new sail for their boat, and was so busy that for the time she forgot her evil arts of magic.

At last everything was ready for Ulysses' departure.

Circe knelt before Ulysses and begged him to spare her

The ship with its white sail lay floating near the shore. The men put on their fresh robes. Then they carried on board jugs of water and wine, sacks of meal, smoked meat, and all the things that they might need on the voyage.

The men seized the oars in their hands. The sail filled with wind, and Ulysses sped away from the island of Circe, favored by her help, toward Ithaca, his home.

Icarus went higher and higher into the heavens

DAEDALUS AND ICARUS

There was once a boy named Icarus who, with his father Daedalus, was imprisoned in a tower on the island of Crete.

From the little window of this lonely tower they could see the blue ocean and watch the gulls and eagles sweep back and forth over the island.

Sometimes a ship sailed out toward other lands, and then Daedalus and Icarus would long for freedom, and wish that they might sail away to Delos and never again see the island of Crete.

Daedalus at last found a way for them to escape from the tower, but they were obliged to hide themselves in the loneliest parts of the island. Minos, the king who had put them in prison, watched the coming and going of all ships, and so Daedalus and Icarus never found courage to go near the harbor where the outgoing galleys lay anchored.

In spite of this, Icarus was almost happy. Besides the blue sea, the ships, and the birds, which he loved to watch, he found shellfish along the shore, crabs among the rocks, and many other curious things.

But Daedalus grew more lonely and miserable and spent all his time watching the gulls as they flew in the air, and planning how he and Icarus might escape from the island.

One day Icarus was throwing stones at the gulls. He killed one of the birds and brought it to his father.

"See how the feathers shine, and how long the wings are!" said the boy.

Daedalus took the bird in his hands and turned it over slowly, examining the wings.

"See," said Icarus, "how the feathers shine, and how long the wings are!"

"Now if we had wings," laughed Icarus, "we could fly away and be free."

For a long time his father sat silent, holding the dead bird. Now and then he looked up and watched other birds as they wheeled in the air over the sea and the island.

At last he thought of a plan and said softly to himself, "We shall have wings, too."

After that, Daedalus was idle no more. He plucked feathers from all the birds that Icarus could kill, and began to make two great wings. He fastened the feathers to a framework with melted wax and threads pulled from his linen mantle.

When these two wings were finished, Daedalus bound them on himself. He rose into the air, waving his arms, now up, now down, and went soaring far out over the water.

Icarus jumped about in delight, and shouted to his father to come back and make another pair of wings so that they might fly away and leave Crete forever.

When Daedalus had finished another pair of wings he bound the smaller pair on his son. Then he warned Icarus not to wander off alone in the air but to follow him closely.

"If you fly too low, the dampness of the sea will make your feathers heavy, and you will sink into the water," said Daedalus. "But if you fly too near the sun the heat will melt the wax and you will fall."

Icarus promised to fly just as his father bade him. Leaping from the highest cliff on the island, they flew away toward Delos.

At first Icarus was obedient and followed close behind his father, but soon in the joy of flying he forgot all that his father had told him, and stretching his arms upward he went higher and higher into the heavens.

Daedalus called to him to return, but the wind passed so swiftly that it carried all sound away, and Icarus could not hear. His wings bore him higher and still higher into the region of the clouds. As he went up and up the air grew warmer and warmer, but he forgot his father's warning and flew on.

At length he saw feathers floating in the air around him and suddenly he remembered his father's warning. He knew that the heat of the sun had melted the wax that held the feathers to the framework.

Finally Icarus felt himself sinking, and fluttered his wings wildly in an effort to fly, but such a storm of feathers swept around him that he could not see.

With a wild cry, turning and whirling through the sky, poor Icarus fell down into the blue waters of the sea—known ever since as the Icarian.

Daedalus heard his cry and flew to the spot, but nothing could be seen of Icarus or his wings except a handful of white feathers which floated on the water.

Sadly the father went on with his journey, and finally reached the shore of a friendly island. There he built a temple to Apollo and hung up his wings as an offering to the god. But ever after he mourned his son, and never again did he try to fly.

POMONA AND VERTUMNUS

Pomona was a nymph who cared for the fruit-bearing trees of the orchards. While her sisters watched over the trees of the forests, Pomona worked among her

The nymph Pomona

apple trees, her pear trees, and her vines. She pruned and tended them from dawn until dark. She led little streams to water their roots, and cut off the long useless shoots.

She trained the grape vines to climb on the trunks of elm trees, so that they spread among the branches until the elms looked as though they were full of blue and amber grapes.

Many lovers came wooing Pomona, the fauns and satyrs and even the god Pan. His legs were like a goat's, but he played such music on his pipes that the nymphs would have no one else to play for their dancing.

Pomona would not think of romance or of wedding anyone. She cared only for her garden and her fruit trees. She loaded her suitors with fruit and sent them all away.

The country people around her, who had gardens of their own, were a great trouble to Pomona. They tried to steal her fruit, and cut shoots from her trees to graft on their own. So she built a high wall around her garden and allowed no suitors or idle country folk to enter through the little gate. After the wall was built her lovers grew discouraged, except one who loved her best of all.

His name was Vertumnus, and he was the god of the changing seasons. He possessed the power of taking any form he wished. Sometimes he pretended to be a reaper, and came to Pomona's gate with a basket of corn to sell. At other times he would carry a pruning hook, and offer to climb the highest trees and to trim the branches which Pomona could not reach. On other days he dressed like a fisherman, and brought her little spotted trout from the streams. In these ways he was allowed

Pan's legs were like a goat's, but he played such music that the nymphs would have no one else to play for their dancing

to come in through the gate and visit Pomona each day, until he grew to love her more than ever.

Once he came as an aged woman, who wore a dark cloak and asked permission to enter the garden and see the fruit. Pomona smiled, and swung the gate wide open. She led the old woman to a grassy bank, and helped her to seat herself beneath a tree. She gathered her largest and reddest apples and offered them to her visitor.

"Do you tend this garden all alone?" asked the woman. "What! have you not chosen a suitor? Do you mean to live alone like this forever?"

Pomona smiled and said that she cared more for her garden than for any youth, and that she liked to live alone. Then the aged stranger pointed to an elm tree on which Pomona had trained her grapes.

"If yonder vine were not twined around the elm," she said, "it would lie on the ground. The sun could never reach the grapes to ripen them and make them grow. You are like the vine, and I will tell you of someone who is like the elm."

The old woman then began to praise Vertumnus.

"No one is stronger, or kinder, or more beautiful than he, and like yourself, he delights in gardening."

She talked so long of this suitor that at length Pomona became interested and almost wished to see him.

Then the old woman craftily began to tell Pomona the story of Anaxarete: how that noble lady scorned her lovers and would marry no one, until at last, in despair, the most ardent of them, named Iphis, killed himself for love of her, and Anaxarete was turned to stone as a punishment for her hardness.

Then, with a laugh, the old woman added, "Beware lest your own coldness bring you a like fate!"

As she spoke her dark cloak fell from her, her wrinkles

Pomona gathered her largest and reddest apples and offered them to her visitor

vanished, her bent shoulders straightened, and Vertumnus himself stood before Pomona.

When he spoke, it was in a voice very different from that of the old woman. Pomona thought it more beautiful than any voice she had ever heard.

As she led him around the garden, Pomona said, "You are indeed like the elm tree, and I would rather be like the vine than like the noble lady Anaxarete."

ATALANTA AND HIPPOMENES

Atalanta was a Greek maiden who could run faster than any one on earth. She could outrun the winds, Boreas and Zephyr. Only Mercury, with his winged sandals, ran more swiftly.

Besides being so fleet-footed, Atalanta was very beautiful, and many Greek youths from every part of the kingdom wished to marry her. But Atalanta did not wish to marry any one and turned them all away, saying, "I shall be the bride only of him who shall outrun me in the race, but death must be the penalty of all who try and fail."

In spite of this hard condition there still were a few brave suitors willing to risk their lives for a chance of winning Atalanta.

For one of the races the runners chose the youth Hippomenes for judge.

Hippomenes felt both pity and scorn for the runners. He thought they were foolish to risk their lives, and bade them go home. He reminded them that the land was full of lovely maidens who were kinder and more gentle than Atalanta.

"But you have not yet seen Atalanta," said one of the suitors to Hippomenes. "You do not know all her beauty and loveliness. See, she comes!"

Hippomenes looked, and saw Atalanta as she drew near. She laid aside her cloak and made ready for the

Hippomenes

race.   For a moment she stood poised like a graceful white bird about to fly.

The suitors who stood beside her trembled with fear and eagerness.

At a word from Hippomenes the runners were off, but at the first step Atalanta flew ahead.   Her tunic fluttered behind her like a banner.   Her hair, loosened from its ribbon, blew about her shoulders in bright waves.

As she ran, Hippomenes thought her very beautiful and became envious of the runner who might win her. He shouted praises when she reached the goal far ahead of her poor suitors.

Hippomenes forgot that the penalty of failure was death. He did not remember the advice he had given the other runners to go home and forget the loveliness of Atalanta. He knew only that he loved her and must himself race with her.

Raising his head toward Mount Olympus, he prayed to Venus, the goddess of love, and asked her to help him.

As he stood beside Atalanta, waiting the signal for the race to start, Venus appeared to him and slipped three golden apples into his hands.

"Throw them one by one in Atalanta's path," whispered Venus.

The goddess was invisible to everyone but Hippomenes. No one saw her as she gave him the apples, nor heard her as she told him what to do with them.

Atalanta looked pityingly at the handsome youth as he stood ready to run. She was sorry for him, and for a moment she hesitated and almost wished that he might win the race.

The signal was given, and Atalanta and Hippomenes flew swiftly over the sand. Atalanta was soon ahead, but Hippomenes, sending up a prayer to Venus, tossed one of his golden apples so that it fell directly in front of Atalanta.

Astonished at the beautiful apple which seemed to fall from nowhere, she stooped to pick it up.

That instant Hippomenes passed her, but Atalanta, holding the apple firmly in her hand, at once darted ahead. Again she outdistanced Hippomenes. Then he threw the second apple.

Atalanta could not pass without picking it up, and then, because of the apple in her other hand, paused a moment longer. When she looked up, Hippomenes was far ahead.

Atalanta stooped to pick up the golden apple

But gaining, she overtook and passed him. Then, just before she reached the goal, he threw the third apple.

"I can win easily," thought Atalanta, "even though I stoop for this other apple." As she was already holding an apple in each hand, she paused just for an instant as she wondered how to grasp the third.

That moment Hippomenes shot past, reaching the goal before Atalanta.

Amid the wild shouts of those who watched, he wrapped the maiden's cloak around her shoulders and led her away. Hippomenes was so happy that he forgot to thank the goddess Venus, who followed them to the marriage feast.

Invisible, she moved among the wedding guests. She saw Atalanta place the golden apples in a bowl of ivory and admire their beauty, but Hippomenes, in his delight, thought no more of the apples or of the goddess who had given them to him.

Venus was angry with Hippomenes for being so thoughtless, and instead of blessing the lovers she caused them to be changed into a lion and a lioness, doomed forever to draw the chariot of Cybele, the mother of Jupiter, through the heavens and over the earth.

CUPID AND APOLLO

Cupid was the baby son of Venus. Although his mother fed him daily with nectar and ambrosia, the food of the gods, he never seemed to grow. The years passed by, and still Cupid remained a tiny, dimpled, laughing child, although he could fly and run wherever he wished and care for himself on earth as well as on Mount Olympus.

When Apollo was not driving his chariot, Cupid loved to follow him around, for he was more fond of Apollo than of any of the other gods. He was much interested in Apollo's bow and arrows and longed to take them in his hand.

Once he saw Apollo take his strongest bow and his sharpest arrows and set out to kill a huge, dark monster called the Python.

The Python was a gloomy creature that breathed heavy black smoke from his nostrils. This filled the air for miles around with darkness, and the shadows were so heavy that no one standing in the valley could see the mountain tops.

As Apollo was the god of light, he did not like the darkness, so he went straight into the shadowy valley, found the terrible Python, and killed him.

Cupid followed him so quietly that Apollo did not know he was there until after the Python was killed, and the darkness had lifted from the valley. Then he saw the boy standing beside him.

"Oh, your arrows are wonderful!" cried Cupid. "Give me one! I'll do anything you say if you will only let me hold your bow."

But Apollo laughed, and taking Cupid's hand in his led him back to his mother.

The baby son of **Venus**

Cupid was greatly disappointed and decided that if he could not have Apollo's bow and arrows he would get some for himself. He knew that almost anything he wished for, Vulcan could make at his anvil, and so one day he asked for a bow like Apollo's, and a quiver of golden arrows.

Vulcan fashioned a little bow, perfect and smooth and slender, and a quiver full of the sharpest, lightest arrows.

Venus, who was watching, gave to these darts a power no large arrows had ever possessed. When any one was

"What have you to do with warlike weapons, saucy boy?"

touched ever so lightly by one of the golden arrows, he at once fell in love with the first person he saw.

Cupid was so delighted with his bow and arrows that he played with them from morning until night.

One day Apollo did not drive his chariot, but left it in the heavens behind the clouds.

"It is a good thing," he said, "for people to have some gray days." So he spent the day hunting through the forest.

In a little glade he came upon Cupid sitting on a mossy rock, playing with his bow and arrows. Apollo was much vexed to think that Cupid could handle so cleverly the same kind of weapons that he had used to kill the Python. He frowned, and spoke harshly to him.

"What have you to do with warlike weapons, saucy boy?" said Apollo. "Put them down and leave such things for grown people."

Cupid was hurt and angry. He had hoped Apollo would praise him for his skill, as Venus had done.

"Your arrows may kill the Python," said Cupid, "but mine shall wound you."

As he spoke he let fly an arrow, which struck Apollo so lightly it barely scratched him. Apollo laughed at him and walked on, not knowing what the wound really meant.

Soon he noticed a beautiful nymph gathering flowers in the forest. Her name was Daphne. Apollo had often seen her before, but she had never seemed so beautiful as now. He ran forward to speak to her. She saw him coming and was startled.

"Let me help you gather flowers," begged Apollo, but Daphne was so shy she ran away. Apollo wanted so much to be with her and talk to her that he ran after her.

Poor Daphne, terrified, ran faster and faster. When she was breathless and could run no more, she cried loudly to Peneus, the river god, for help.

Daphne was so shy she ran away

Peneus was her father and, hearing his daughter's voice from far away, he thought she was in some terrible danger. Swiftly he sent his magic power over the forest, and to protect her changed her into a tree.

Daphne's feet clung to the earth and took root. She felt the rough bark creeping over her shoulders and limbs. From her arms sprang branches, and her hands were filled with leaves. When Apollo reached out his hand to touch her, the fair maiden had vanished. In her place stood a beautiful laurel tree.

"What have I done?" mourned Apollo.

He was so grieved and sad because he had brought this change on Daphne that he stayed by the tree all the afternoon, talking to it and begging Daphne to forgive him.

He asked for some of her laurel leaves that he might wear them on his head. Daphne shook her branches, and a little shower of leaves fell around Apollo. By this he knew that Daphne forgave him, and he gathered the leaves tenderly in his hands and wove them into a wreath.

Throwing aside a drooping wreath of flowers which he wore about his brow, Apollo placed the laurel on his head, where it remained forever fresh and green.

Pluto seized Proserpina by the wrist

PROSERPINA AND PLUTO

Pluto was god of Erebus, the world that lies beneath the ground. In his realm all was dark, misty, and gloomy. There was no sunshine there, nor any light except the glow of fires. Instead of blue sky overhead, he had only a roof of damp and dripping earth. There were no gay-colored flowers in his kingdom, nor tall branching trees, nor green grass.

In some places the dripping water mingled with rust-colored lime from the earth, and hardened into all sorts of shapes. It made columns and arches and mounds, or hung like icicles in long, thin pendants from the roofs of Pluto's many caverns. There were black marble rocks in Erebus, and deep, dark lakes.

It would have been a dreary place for an earth child, but Pluto thought his kingdom the most beautiful in the world.

He thought his caves hung with lime crystals far lovelier than forests of birch trees. He liked the noiseless peace of the dim caverns. No songs of birds, no rustle of wind among the trees, disturbed their quiet. Only at times he heard far off the barking of Cerberus, who guarded the entrance to his kingdom.

To drive away the dampness in the caves, Pluto lit many fires. Their flickering flames made the lime crystals sparkle and glimmer on the dark waters of the lakes. These fires were silent, too. They never crackled cheerfully as earth fires do.

The god of this strange, quiet land was content to stay in his own kingdom and seldom journeyed to the earth, which seemed a noisy place after the deep silence of Erebus.

Pluto, the god of this strange quiet land, was content to stay in his own kingdom

But once Jupiter imprisoned four great giants in a cavern in Mount Aetna. In their anger the giants stamped their feet and shook the earth, raging back and forth and beating on the walls of their prison, or heaving their mighty shoulders against the sides of the cavern until the mountain trembled.

Far off in his kingdom under the ground Pluto heard these strange rumblings and feared that from the shock the surface of the earth might crack and the light of day break through.

So, mounting his chariot drawn by four black horses, he journeyed swiftly up to earth and rode here and there to see how much damage had been done by the angry giants.

He found temples overturned, trees uprooted, and rocks thrown about as though some great earthquake had shaken the land, but no cracks deep enough to disturb the gloom of Erebus.

Pluto was preparing to return home, for the light of the sun was painful to his eyes, and he did not like the strange perfume of the earth flowers nor the sound of wind in the trees. But Cupid, that mischievous god of love, had other plans for Pluto.

He drew his bow, wounding the god of darkness with one of those arrows which cause the wounded one to love the first person he meets.

Pluto had just grasped the reins of his four black horses to turn them homeward, when he saw Proserpina, the daughter of Ceres, with half a dozen nymphs, dancing across the valley. Proserpina's hair floated behind her, bright as a flame of golden fire, and her eyes were as black as Pluto's lakes. She came nearer, gathering flowers and twining them into garlands.

The god of the dark kingdom stepped from his chariot and left it hidden among the trees. His cloak waved about him in many points and folds, thin and fluttering like a garment of smoke. Little tongues of fire rose from his crown and flickered above his forehead.

Proserpina and the nymphs saw him and drew back in alarm. Pluto strode toward them and seized Proserpina by the wrist. He did not woo her gently and kindly as lovers do. He said nothing at all, but lifted her in his arms and carried her off into the forest. Stepping into his chariot, he seized the reins with one hand, and held Proserpina with the other. The four black horses sprang forward with a bound, galloping madly away toward the river Cyane.

Proserpina screamed for help. She cried to Ceres, her mother, but Pluto urged on his horses, and the chariot dashed away still faster.

When they reached the edge of the river Cyane, Pluto commanded the waters to open so that he might pass, but the river nymph saw that Proserpina was being carried away, and refused to help Pluto or make a pathway for him to cross.

Then in anger Pluto struck the ground with his mighty three-pronged spear, and the earth itself opened. The horses plunged downward, and with the chariot rattling from side to side, disappeared in the darkness.

Now, far off, Ceres had heard Proserpina's cry as Pluto carried her away. A sharp pain shot through the mother's heart, and like a bird she flew through forest and valley, seeking Proserpina. She climbed mountains and crossed rivers, asking everyone she met for tidings of Proserpina, but neither man nor god would tell her where Pluto had carried her daughter.

A long, dark cloak hid Ceres' face and the brightness of her hair. No one who saw her then would have known

A long dark cloak hid the brightness of Ceres' hair

that she was the glowing goddess of the harvest. For many days she wandered over the earth, refusing in her sorrow to taste either ambrosia or nectar.

Once, as she sat on a stone resting beside a well, the four daughters of Celeus, running and leaping like young gazelles, came to fill their pitchers.

*The four daughters of Celeus, running and leaping like young gazelles, came to
fill their pitchers at the well*

They saw the aged woman at the spring. Her head
was bent in sorrow, and her dark mantle spoke of mourning. They touched her gently on the shoulder and asked
her why she grieved, but Ceres did not tell them or let
them know that she was a goddess. She let them think
she was only an aged woman in trouble.

When their pitchers were filled, they put their arms
around Ceres and led her home. Everyone in the house
of Celeus was so gentle and kind that Ceres found comfort in her sorrow.

Celeus had an infant son who fell ill while Ceres rested
in his home. The goddess nursed the little boy and gave

him heavenly gifts, so that he grew in strength and beauty and wisdom.

Celeus and his family begged the visitor to live with them always, but Ceres wandered on, still seeking for Proserpina.

At last she came to the banks of the river Cyane, but the river nymph, fearing the anger of Pluto, dared not tell Ceres where the missing Proserpina was hidden.

The nymphs shivered and wrapped their robes around them

Now it happened that as Pluto's horses had dashed down into the earth, Proserpina's girdle, loosened by her struggle to free herself, fell from the chariot and lay on the river bank.

The river nymph now took this girdle and floated it to where Ceres stood mourning at the water's edge.

Ceres saw it, and now her grief was more terrible than ever. She took away her blessing from the earth and cast an evil spell on the fruits and crops.

The leaves of the trees lost their green and began to fall in clouds of yellow. The blue sky grew angry and gray, and a cold wind swept over the earth. The nymphs shivered and wrapped their thin robes around them.

Everything became dry and withered, and famine and sickness and grief were over the whole earth.

Then the fountain, Arethusa, spoke to Ceres and told her where Proserpina was. "I come from far down in the earth," sang the fountain. "My waters have trickled through the realms of Pluto. I have seen your daughter. I have seen Proserpina, the beautiful, the bright, sitting on a black marble throne, queen of the spirits which wander silently between the crystal pillars and the flickering fires, and float over the lakes from which my waters rise."

When Ceres heard this, she raised her arms to Jupiter and begged him to return Proserpina to the earth.

"Never again," she cried, "will I make the corn grow or the ripening grain bend in golden waves. Unless my daughter is restored to me, never again will I watch over the harvest. The fruits of the earth shall remain withered, and man die from hunger."

Jupiter feared that Ceres would do as she threatened, so he sent Mercury, the speedy messenger, to fly swiftly to Pluto, and bid him release Proserpina.

Mercury, the speedy messenger of the gods

"But if she has eaten in Erebus even I cannot take her from Pluto," said Jupiter.

When Mercury went down into the kingdom of darkness, he took Spring with him. They flew over the river Styx and passed Cerberus, the three-headed dog. When Cerberus, his three great jaws wide open, sprang at them, Spring loosed her mantle and shook such a shower of white petals in his face that he could not see. His mouths were filled with them, and they clung to the lashes of his eyes. Some fell into the river Styx and floated on the dark water.

"They are like the fair queen, Proserpina, on her black marble throne," said Charon, the boatman.

"Such a dreary place to keep the daughter of Ceres!" thought Mercury, as they flew through the gloomy caverns and passages toward Pluto's palace.

Soon Pluto began to notice a faint fragrance which reminded him of the earth world above. He frowned, and hurried to the doors of his palace. Proserpina felt the mild warmth and followed.

They saw Mercury approaching, with Spring floating at his side. "Rejoice, O daughter of Ceres," said Mercury, "for Jupiter bids you return to earth, which lies brown and barren because of grief over your loss."

Pluto frowned more fiercely than ever. "She has eaten six seeds of a pomegranate," he said. "The fates decree that whoever eats in Erebus never may leave."

"But only six little seeds!" begged Proserpina. "There are twice six months in the year. Only let me see my mother! Let me feel the warm sunshine and soft winds, and gather flowers again, and I will come back to you!"

Pluto had grown to love Proserpina dearly. He could not bear to lose her forever, yet he wished her to be happy. So he agreed to let her go back to her mother for six months of the year, but the other six she promised to spend with him.

With Spring on one side and Mercury on the other, Proserpina journeyed up to earth, where Ceres awaited her.

As the ground opened to let them out, the cold winds hurried away beyond the sea. Ceres dropped her mantle

"Proserpina has eaten six seeds of a pomegranate"

of gray and laughed with joy to hold her daughter once more in her arms. The bare branches burst into bud, and tiny leaves sprang from every twig. Starry white flowers sprinkled the moss, and the perfume of Spring filled the forest.

Mercury flew back to Mount Olympus, but Spring began her journey over the earth to star the fields with blossoms and carry the tidings that Proserpina had come back.

CUPID AND PSYCHE

Once there lived in Greece a blue-eyed princess named Psyche. She was so fair, so beautiful, that strangers came from far-away countries to look at her and scatter roses in her path. When she smiled, even the immortals were delighted as they watched her from the heights of Mount Olympus.

Only one grew angry when Psyche was praised. Venus, the goddess of beauty, looked down at her temples on the earth and saw that they were empty. The young men who should have brought garlands for her altars were casting chaplets of roses at Psyche's feet and singing hymns of praise to her. So Venus called her son Cupid and sent him to wound Psyche with one of his golden arrows.

Cupid sharpened his weapons as his mother bade him, flew down to the palace where Psyche lay asleep, and lightly touched his golden arrow to her side. At once Psyche awoke and turned her eyes toward Cupid, although she could not see him, for he was invisible.

She was so wonderfully fair that Cupid's heart beat wildly as he bent over her, and a weakness came over him such as he had never felt before. His hand slipped, and he wounded himself with his own arrow. That moment Cupid fell in love with Psyche, a mortal maiden.

Troubled and bewildered, he flew back to Olympus and praised the lovely Psyche to his mother. Now Venus

As she lay asleep, Cupid lightly touched his golden arrow to Psyche's side

was more angry with Psyche than before. By her arts she turned all of Psyche's lovers away from her, and she forbade Cupid ever to enter the palace of the blue-eyed princess or to look upon her again.

Soon Psyche's elder sisters were married to great princes, but no lover sought Psyche, although she grew more and more lovely. At length her parents, feeling sure that the gods were angry, journeyed to the temple of Apollo to seek advice of the oracle.

"The maiden is to be the bride of an immortal lover," the oracle replied, "a monster of such power that neither gods nor men can resist him. He awaits her on the top of the mountain."

This answer filled the king and queen and all their people with terror, but Psyche robed herself in her most beautiful garments and, followed by her parents and friends, ascended the mountain. At the top they bade her good-by and left her there alone.

While Psyche stood on the mountain top, weeping and trembling with fright, Zephyr, the west wind, lifted her gently in his arms and carried her to a flowery valley below. Near by in a grove of tall and stately trees she saw a wonderful white palace, and in an open place fountains played amid blossoming branches. As she drew nearer to the palace she knew it was the home of an immortal, so great was its splendor. Golden pillars supported the high-arched roof, and paintings and sculpture ornamented the walls.

As she walked through the lovely rooms a voice all sweetness and gentleness spoke to her, "Fair Princess, all that you behold is yours. Command us, we are your servants." Filled with wonder and delight, Psyche looked about in all directions, but saw no one. The voice continued, "Here is your chamber, and your bed of down; here is your bath, and in the adjoining alcove there is food."

Psyche bathed, and put on the lovely garments prepared for her, then seated herself on a chair of carved ivory. At once there floated to its place before her a table covered with golden dishes and with the finest food. Although she could see no one, invisible hands served her, and unseen musicians played on lutes and sang to her.

For a long time Psyche did not see the master of the palace. He visited her only in the night time, going away before morning dawned, but his voice was gentle and tender, not at all like that of a monster. Psyche some-

Zephyr, the west wind, lifted her gently in his arms and carried her to a flowery valley

times begged him to stay through the day, but always he replied, "If you beheld my face, perhaps you would fear me, perhaps adore me, but I would rather you should love me as an equal than adore me as a god."

Psyche next begged her husband that her sisters might visit her. Although Cupid knew there would be trouble if they entered his home, he yielded to Psyche's pleading, and Zephyr was sent to bring them across the mountain and down to the enchanted valley.   At first they were happy to see their young sister and to find her safe, but soon, seeing all the splendor in Psyche's palace, envy sprang up in their hearts. They questioned her rudely concerning her husband.

"Love cannot dwell with suspicion," Cupid said sadly

"Is he not some dreadful monster," they asked, "some dragon, who will at length devour you?   Remember what the oracle said!"

Before their visit was over they begged Psyche to look at Cupid as he lay asleep.   They urged her to carry a lamp and a great knife, so that she might cut off his head if he were indeed a dragon.   Psyche promised to do so, and her sisters departed.

Psyche hid the lamp and knife where she could find them quickly. At midnight, when her lord was sleeping, she arose, lit her lamp, and bent over his couch. The light showed her, not a dragon nor a monster, but a youth more beautiful than any she had ever seen, with golden curls falling over his pillow, and white wings gleaming softly, like pearl and crystal.

As she turned to put out the lamp a drop of burning oil fell upon his shoulder. Cupid awoke and, looking at her sorrowfully, spread his shining wings and flew out of the window. Psyche held wide her arms and, standing on the ledge of the window, tried to follow him. But Zephyr did not receive her, and she fell.

For an instant Cupid turned back to her. "Love cannot dwell with suspicion," he said sadly, and flew away.

As Psyche lay weeping, the palace and gardens and fountains vanished, and she found herself again in her own land. Sadly she went to the palace and told her sisters what had happened. She would not stay with her sisters, but wandered away to seek her beloved. Day and night, without food or rest, she journeyed over the wildest mountains. At last she saw a beautiful temple gleaming on a hill.

"Perhaps he is there," she thought, and climbed breathlessly to the hilltop. She entered the temple. Before the altar of Ceres she saw sheaves of barley, ears of corn, piles of grain, and sickles and rakes thrown down in careless disorder by the tired harvesters.

Psyche stooped and carefully piled the grain and the sheaves of barley. She gathered the sickles and rakes and placed them on the steps of the temple, where the reapers might find them in the morning. Then, when she had swept the floor, she seated herself to rest.

Ceres, the goddess of this temple, was pleased at Psyche's service, and advised her to go at once to Venus, offer to serve her, and beg for pity and forgiveness. When Psyche reached the court of Venus, she knelt before the goddess and promised to serve her in whatever way Venus might wish if only she might be allowed to see Cupid and finally be forever near him. Venus was still angry with Psyche, so she set her the most difficult tasks she could find.

She led Psyche to a storehouse where there were great piles of wheat, barley, millet, lentils, and beans, which Venus kept for her doves.

"First sort these grains," said Venus. "Put each kind in a separate bag, and finish the task by nightfall."

Psyche sat down on the floor of the storeroom and gazed hopelessly at the piles of grain. She knew she could not finish the task before evening, nor even if she toiled for many days. But Cupid, who still loved her, had been listening, and he now sent those tireless little workers, the ants, to help. They came marching from their hills in long black lines and crawled up on the piles of grain. Then, each carrying one kernel at a time, they patiently sorted the piles and filled the bags before evening.

When Venus returned she found everything in order. But when she saw that Psyche's task was completed, she was more angry than ever, for she felt sure that Cupid had

Venus commanded Psyche to go to the realm of Proserpina and Pluto

helped her. Throwing a piece of black bread to Psyche for her supper, she left her.

The next morning Venus sent Psyche to bring a sample of golden wool from each of the sheep in a flock that fed across a near-by river. As Psyche stood on the river bank wondering how she might cross, the river god bade the rushes and reeds murmur softly and tell her she must not try to cross in the morning, nor venture among the angry rams until the noon shadows lay deep and the sheep went to rest in the shade.

Psyche waited on the river bank until noontime, when the sheep were drowsing in the shade, and then crossed safely over. She gathered the golden fleece from the bushes where it was clinging, and carried it back to Venus. But Venus gave her no praise, only another crust for her supper.

The third day Venus commanded Psyche to go to the realm of Proserpina and Pluto, and say to Proserpina, "My mistress Venus begs you to send her a little of your beauty, for in caring for her wounded son she has lost some of her own."

Now Psyche was more hopeless than ever, for she was sure she never could travel on foot to Erebus, where Proserpina dwelt. But when she was most down-hearted a friendly voice explained to her how she might safely pass the dangers on her way. It told her how to weave a charm about Cerberus, the three-headed dog, and how to prevail on Charon, the aged boatman of the river Styx, to row her across the stream and back again. It warned her especially not to open the jar in which she was to carry the precious beauty.

The voice reminded her of Cupid, whom she had lost. It was tender, like the voice of her lover, and gentle. So courage came into her heart, and she set forth, carrying a golden jar in her hands. She walked through a dark cave and on through a narrow passageway, dripping with water, until she came to a wider entrance where Cerberus, with his three great heads, barked fiercely and shook the earth with his growls. Trembling, she kept her face toward him, talking gently to him as she drew nearer.

His barking ceased, and his growling grew fainter and fainter. When she reached him he lay down and thumped the ground with his tail, just as the friendly dogs of the earth always did when Psyche passed by them.

Charon ferried Psyche across the dark water

At the river Styx the aged boatman took her hand and led her to the boat. He ferried her across the dark water, and Psyche went on her way to Proserpina's throne, where she delivered the message from Venus.

When Proserpina had filled the golden jar, Psyche again returned and crossed the river with Charon. Passing the dreadful Cerberus, she at last found herself outside the cave in the sunshine. As she rested on a grassy bank she looked longingly at the little jar.

"What harm can it do," Psyche thought, "if I just peep in and take a tiny bit of the beauty for myself, so that when Cupid again sees me I shall be even more lovely?"

So she took off the lid, and at once up into her face flew clouds of strange fragrance. She could not see the jar or even the grass around her, but fell back asleep. Cupid, still invisible, had been waiting and watching at the entrance of the cavern for her return. He flew to her side, and gathering the clouds of sleepy magic he placed them again in the jar and wakened Psyche.

"Again," he said, "you have almost perished because of your curiosity."

Psyche was so happy to be with Cupid that she would have forgotten to finish her errand. But Cupid knew that Venus must be obeyed, and he sent Psyche on with the jar while he himself flew to Jupiter and begged that Psyche might be made immortal so that she might stay with him forever.

Jupiter granted Cupid's plea, and sent Mercury, messenger of the gods, to carry Psyche to Mount Olympus, where the gods were waiting to welcome her.

Hebe, the cupbearer of the gods

A glorious haze of light, as many-colored as a rainbow, hid the throne of Jupiter from Psyche's sight, for being mortal she might not look on the ruler of the gods.

Hebe, the cupbearer of the immortals, advanced to meet her, carrying in her hand a goblet of ambrosia, which she gave to Psyche. The fragrant liquid not only refreshed Psyche but bestowed upon her the gift of immortality. Immediately after she had emptied the goblet her weariness fell from her, her body felt new strength, her heart was filled with new gladness, and her face and form appeared more lovely than ever.

The haze of light rolled away from Jupiter's throne, and Psyche beheld the ruler of the gods. Kneeling before him, she gave him humble thanks.

Venus, feeling forgiveness in her heart, now came forward to embrace Psyche and give her to Cupid for his bride.

Ever after, on the sunny summit of Mount Olympus, Cupid and Psyche lived together in happiness.

ORPHEUS AND EURYDICE

Once on a spring morning, Orpheus sat on a hilltop high above the world, singing and playing his lute. He sang of the spring flowers and the south wind in the trees. He made rippling melodies that sounded like the waters of fountains and tiny streams. But above all these he sang of Eurydice and his love for her.

As he played, the tall treetops bowed their heads to listen, and daffodils raised their budded stems and opened wide to hear him.

Pan and all the satyrs came running and leaping through the woods. The centaurs, who were half man and half horse, smiled to hear the music. They thought such things as mortals do in spring time, although their four feet tingled with the happiness which horses feel when they gallop over the green grass in April.

The nymphs wakened in wooded bowers and, fastening their tunics on their shoulders, hurried out to listen.

Eurydice herself opened her eyes and thought sweetly, "It is Orpheus." She dressed, and twined a garland in her hair, then ran toward the hilltop where he sang.

From all sides came birds and nymphs, fauns and dryads, all hurrying toward Orpheus. Little spotted snakes crawled up from their homes in the ground and wriggled through the grass. The tiny orange-colored serpent, whose bite means death, rose also and lifted his head to listen.

Now Aristaeus, the keeper of bees, came running. His garden lay far away from the hill, but he had heard the faint echo of Orpheus' lute.

He saw Eurydice and called to her to wait for him, but she ran on. Aristaeus tried to overtake her, but Eurydice ran more rapidly than ever. She did not want to talk to Aristaeus, but cared only to find Orpheus and sit beside him as he played.

She turned back to look at Aristaeus as he followed. At that moment she set her foot on the poisonous serpent which wriggled across her path. A fiery tongue darted out and struck Eurydice's heel, and she fell to the grass.

As Aristaeus drew nearer, he saw the earth opened. He saw the river Styx, and heard the far-off barking of Cerberus. Charon, the hoary boatman, waited to row her across.

Eurydice floated away. Still looking back toward the hill where Orpheus played, she put her hand in Charon's and disappeared across the dark water into the realm of Erebus.

On the hilltop Orpheus sang and watched for Eurydice, wondering why she did not come. Every other nymph and dryad, and indeed all the living things of the forest had gathered to listen, except Eurydice, his beloved. At length he saw Aristaeus come stumbling and weeping up the hillside.

"Eurydice is dead," said Aristaeus, "and gone with Charon across the river."

"Then I will follow," said Orpheus.

He touched his lute, and at the sound of his music sadness swept over the earth. The centaurs wept and walked away. The animals of the forest slunk back to their dens.

Orpheus touched his lute, and sadness swept over the earth

The nymphs and dryads threw themselves on the grass and mourned. The rocks shed tears, and the earth, hearing the sad music, opened the same crevice through which Eurydice had passed and allowed Orpheus to follow.

At the sound of his lute, Charon came ferrying back over the water and rowed Orpheus across to the land of the shades. Cerberus ceased his barking and lay down as Orpheus passed.

Through the long avenues under the earth and through the great caverns of Erebus he wandered, seeking Eurydice and playing on his lute. Never before had such sounds stolen through the quiet kingdom of Pluto. The shades forgot their drowsy sadness and came thronging to hear.

Through the long avenues under the earth wandered Orpheus

Again they remembered the earth, and the sunshine and rain, and the sadness of loving.

Past the dark lakes and under arches of crystals came Eurydice

Passing through crowds of ghosts, Orpheus came to the throne of Pluto and Proserpina, and sang of his sorrow:

"O gods of the underworld, to whom all who live must come, hear my words. I am Orpheus, son of Apollo, and I seek my beloved, Eurydice. Let me lead her to the earth, or I myself will remain here, for I cannot return alone."

As his fingers strayed over the lute strings, such sorrowful music spread through Erebus that the shades began to weep. The daughters of Danaus rested from their task of drawing water in a sieve. Tantalus, who was doomed to eternal thirst, for a moment forgot his misery and listened to the song of Orpheus. For the first time, the cheeks of the Furies were wet with tears.

Proserpina's heart was filled with pity, and Pluto himself could not resist Orpheus' prayer. They sent for Eurydice, who was in a distant cavern with the newly arrived shades.

Past the dark lakes and under arches of hanging crystals she came, trying to find her way toward the music which she heard from far off.

Orpheus was allowed to take her away with him, but Pluto warned him that he must not look at her or speak to her until they reached the upper air. So Orpheus went ahead, and Eurydice followed close behind him.

Through dark passages and by the shores of many lakes they hurried without a word, until they reached the banks of the river Styx. Here the aged boatman ferried them across. Now they ran more swiftly than before in their eagerness to reach the open air.

When they had come nearly to the entrance, Orpheus felt a terrible fear that Eurydice might not be following. Forgetting the warning of Pluto, he turned and saw her lovely face smiling at him. Then instantly, with a cry of farewell, Eurydice was borne away.

Orpheus was allowed to take Eurydice away, but he must not look at her or speak to her until they reached the upper air

Their arms reached toward each other, but embraced only the empty air. Orpheus could hear the faint sweet call of her voice as she vanished forever into the depths of Erebus.

He would have turned back and followed her, but Charon would not row him across the Styx.

For seven whole days Orpheus waited, pleading with Charon, but the grim boatman still refused. Though Orpheus played on his lute, and moved oaks and mountains with the power of his music, he could not prevail upon the gods of Erebus again, nor could he enter the dark kingdom a second time.

The rest of his life he lived in sadness and loneliness, only waiting for the time when he might die and join Eurydice.

At last death came to Orpheus. Charon ferried him across the river Styx to where Eurydice awaited him. Nor were they ever separated again, but hand in hand roamed forever through the shadowy land of Erebus.

PHAETON AND THE CHARIOT
OF THE SUN

Once, on their way from school, two Greek boys began to quarrel.

"You are nobody!" said one. "Who is your father?"

"Is Apollo indeed my father?"

"My father is Phoebus Apollo, god of the sun. He drives the four great horses of the day. He lights the earth and the heavens with his light, and I, Phaeton, am his son."

His comrade laughed loudly at his boast. He could not believe that the father of Phaeton, his schoolmate, was Apollo, the god of the sun. He called the other boys together and told them Phaeton's story. They crossed

"O light of the boundless world, Phoebus, my father!"

their fingers at him and made all manner of fun of the boy for pretending to be the son of a god.

Phaeton, his cheeks flaming with anger, ran home and burst into his mother's chamber. He told her what had happened.

"Is Apollo indeed my father?" he demanded. "How can I be sure, how can I find proof?"

Clymene, his mother, smiled and drew him to her side. She told him again of the glories of Apollo, as she had often told him before.

"Soon," she said, "you will wish to go yourself to the land where the sun rises and find him where he sits on his throne of light, with the four seasons beside him and the hours and the days grouped near by. Why not journey there and see for yourself, and find proof that Apollo is your father?"

So, although Clymene grieved to have him leave her, she made him ready for the journey and bade him a loving farewell.

He traveled many days through gray and barren lands, over mountains and across streams, until at length he reached the land of the rising sun and saw afar off the flaming light which glowed about the palace of his father.

As he drew nearer he saw that the columns of the palace were of gold and ivory, upholding a jeweled roof. The steps leading to the entrance shone with every kind of precious stone.

Phaeton entered the palace, and there on his golden throne in the great central hall, surrounded by a wonderful white light, he saw Apollo, clad in pale purple, beautiful and dazzling.

On the sun god's right stood Spring, her head crowned with flowers, and Summer, with poppies in her hair. On his left stood Autumn, wreathed in grapes, and aged Winter, bowed over with the weight of ice and snow.

Apollo looked down and saw the boy as he drew near, his hand shielding his eyes. He knew in a moment that this was his son Phaeton, and laid aside the rays that shone about his head, so that Phaeton might not be blinded by their brightness.

"O light of the boundless world, Phoebus, my father!" Phaeton cried. "If you are indeed my parent, give me some proof by which I may be known as your son."

Apollo stretched out his hand to Phaeton and drew him nearer. He looked at him, so straight and brave and young, and the sun god was proud of him.

"My son," he said, "for proof, ask of me what you wish and it shall be given."

Phaeton at once thought of the chariot of the sun. He pictured himself riding across the sky holding the reins of his father's horses. He imagined the amazement of his friends if they could see him.

"Let me for one day drive the chariot of the sun," he answered. "Let me ride from morning until evening through the clouds in your chariot, holding the reins of your four horses."

Apollo was sorry that he had made Phaeton so rash a promise, and begged him to choose something else. He

The horses left the traveled road and dashed headlong in among the stars

reminded the boy that he was not yet grown, and that he was only mortal. He told of the dreadful dangers that every day surrounded the chariot on both its upward and its downward path.

"The first part of the way," he said, "is so steep that the horses can barely climb it, and the last part descends so rapidly that I can hardly hold them. Besides, the heaven itself is always turning, hurrying with it the stars, and always I am afraid lest it sweep me from the chariot and carry the horses from the road. The way leads through the abode of frightful monsters. You must pass the horns of the Bull, the Lion's jaws, the Scorpion, and the Crab.

"O Phaeton," he begged, "look around the world and choose whatever you wish that is precious, whether in the sea or in the midst of the earth, and it shall be yours; but give up this longing to drive my chariot, which can mean only death to you, and destruction."

"No," said Phaeton, "I do not care for anything either in the sea or on the earth. I want only to drive the chariot of Phoebus, my father."

So Phoebus Apollo sadly led the way to the chariot. It was of gold, with a seat of jewels, and around it flamed such a blaze of light that for a moment Phaeton feared to go nearer, it seemed so fiery and scorching.

Rosy-fingered Dawn threw open the silver doors of the East, and there before him Phaeton saw the stars fading away, and the moon, her nightly journey finished, hurrying from the sky. The four great chargers were led from their stalls, and Phaeton cried out in delight as he saw their arched necks and stamping feet. Fire poured from their nostrils, and their hoofs were shod with light.

Phoebus bathed the boy's face with a powerful oil so that he would not be burned, set the rays of the sun on his head, and bade him hold tight to the reins, keep to the middle of the road, and follow the tracks of the wheels.

"Go not too high," he warned, "or you will burn the heavenly dwellings; nor too low, or you will set the earth on fire."

Phaeton joyfully grasped the reins and, holding his head high with delight and pride, rode into the purple path of the morning sky.

The Scorpion reached his great claws toward the chariot

The horses darted forward with mighty strength and scattered the clouds. Soon they felt that the touch on the reins was not their master's, but a lighter one, and that the chariot itself was not so heavy. So, filling the air with their fiery snorting, they sped on faster and faster, while Phaeton tried to hold them back.

They left the traveled road and dashed headlong in among the stars. Phaeton was borne along like the petal of a flower by the wind, and knew not how to guide his fiery steeds. Looking down, he saw the earth spread-

His hair on fire, Phaeton fell headlong like a streak of lightning

ing below, and his knees grew weak with fright. He wished that he had never left his mother or asked to drive the chariot of the sun.

Around him on every side were the monsters of the sky. The Scorpion reached his great claws toward the chariot as it passed, and Phaeton dropped the reins. The horses galloped off into unknown regions of the sky, now high up toward the abode of the gods, now downward, so close to the earth that the mountains caught fire, the Alps covered with snow grew hot, and the Apennines flamed.

The earth cracked open. Grassy plains were scorched into deserts, Even the sea shrank, and the fishes and water nymphs hurried down to the deepest parts of the ocean.

So terrible was the heat that Mother Earth cried out to Jupiter, "O ruler of the gods, I can no more supply fruits for men, or herbage for cattle, and my brother Ocean suffers with me. Your own heaven is smoking, and your clouds are on fire. If sea, earth, and heaven burn, we fall again into Chaos. Oh, take thought for our deliverance!"

Then Jupiter mounted the tower on Olympus, from which he shook his thunderbolts and his forked lightning. He hurled a mighty bolt at the chariot and poured rain on the smoking earth until the fires were extinguished.

Poor Phaeton, still clinging to the reeling chariot as it swayed across the sky, was struck by Jupiter's thunderbolt and, his hair on fire, fell headlong like a streak of lightning into the river Eridanus, which soothed him and cooled his burning body.

ARCAS AND CALLISTO

There was once in Arcady a fair and gentle nymph named Callisto. The gods had given her many graces and blessings, the greatest of which was her little son Arcas.

Jupiter himself was so pleased with Callisto's goodness and charm that he came often to visit her and watch her at play with Arcas.

These visits filled Juno with anger, and she planned a cruel punishment for Callisto. Wrapping herself in her long gray cloak, the goddess descended from Mount Olympus, passing through the dusky cloud gates down to the earth. She found Callisto just awakening in her forest bower. Her rosy little son Arcas lay asleep beside her.

Juno made herself invisible and waited until Callisto rose and came out of her bower. Then, touching the nymph on her shoulder, she changed her into a great furry bear.

Poor Callisto saw her slender white fingers change into long claws, and her arms grow black and hairy. She fell to the earth and began to walk on all fours. Then Juno returned to Mount Olympus.

When the other nymphs came to seek Callisto, they could not find her. Only a great hairy bear stood in the entrance to the bower, trying to fondle the little boy Arcas and turn him over with her paw as he lay asleep.

The nymphs drove the bear away, although it looked back at them sadly as they flung sticks and stones after it.

Thinking that the bear had killed Callisto, the maidens took Arcas to a shepherd, who loved and cared for him.

A great hairy bear was trying to fondle the little Arcas

Sometimes the shepherd saw a bear prowling around his hut, trying to look in at the window or the door. He drove the beast away and flung his spear at it, until at last the poor thing was afraid to come near the hut, and stayed at the edge of the woods, watching always for a sight of the little boy who lived with the shepherd.

Sometimes Arcas would stray near the forest, gathering flowers or playing with his ball. Then the bear would run to greet him, growling softly and kindly, but the child always screamed and ran back.

When Arcas grew old enough, the shepherd taught him to use a spear and took him hunting.

As long as the shepherd was with Arcas, Callisto hid herself. But one day the youth came alone, holding his spear in his hand and feeling very brave and proud.

Callisto stood on her hind legs and came toward him, holding out her great paws, trying to speak and tell him that she was his mother, enchanted into this wild beast. Arcas saw her coming and raised his spear to kill the bear, but something held his arm and the spear was not thrown.

Arcas playing with his ball

Jupiter, watching over Arcas on his first hunt, had seen beneath the bear's fur and hairy paws, and knew that this was the nymph Callisto.

Jupiter stayed the hand of Arcas, and took away his spear

He stayed the hand of Arcas, and took away his spear. He could not undo Juno's evil work, so he changed Arcas into a young bear. At once he understood his mother and knew what she had been trying to tell him.

Callisto and Arcas would have been happy to roam the woods together, but Jupiter thought of something far better for them. As the Great Bear and the Little Bear he took them up into the heavenly realms and gave them the sky for their playground.

Juno was angry when she saw the new constellations placed among the stars, but she could not interfere because Jupiter was the ruler of the heavens.

So she went to Neptune, the god who ruled the sea, and made him promise her that he would forbid the bears to rest like the other stars beneath the ocean.

Juno was angry when she saw the new constellations

And so the Big Bear and the Little Bear, always moving around near the Pole, stay forever in the sky, but being near each other they are happy, and have learned to rest content among the clouds.

THE GOLDEN TOUCH

There was once a very rich king named Midas. The columns of his palace were inlaid with gold, and his treasure room was filled with jewels, yet he was not satisfied. He longed for greater wealth. He did not care for music or flowers, or indeed for anything else except his beautiful little daughter and his riches.

Midas wished to give his daughter, Marigold, the finest dresses ever made, the most beautiful beads and jeweled bands for her hair. This was one reason why he longed to have gold and riches. But Marigold loved to wear a short white frock, and to go barefoot over the grass with only a band of ribbon on her head.

She liked to feel the cool wind blow through her curls; she loved roses and violets much better than jewels. Sometimes she begged King Midas to leave his treasure room, where he liked to sit, to walk in the woods with her.

"The birds are singing," she would say, "and the very first anemones are in bloom."

But Midas would pat her head and tell her to run out and play—just as all busy fathers have told their little girls ever since.

One day, as Midas sat counting his riches, a stranger walked into the room and touched him on the shoulder. Vines twined around the visitor's head, and a leopard skin hung from his shoulders.

"Who are you?" cried Midas in alarm, "and how did you pass the guards?"

"I am Bacchus," said the stranger. "I have come to

Marigold the little daughter of King Midas

thank you. Not long ago you were kind to my old teacher, Silenus. The gods do not forget such things."

Then Midas remembered that one evening an aged man had stumbled into the palace. Midas had given him shelter and food and fresh clothing. In the morning the King had sent him on his way with a companion to guide him.

Midas rose to his feet—as even a royal mortal should stand in the presence of the gods—and bowed low to Bacchus, inviting him to be seated. Bacchus looked at the chair inlaid with gold. He saw the table strewn with jewels and coins and glittering bowls. He shuddered and moved farther away from Midas.

"I cannot stay in this room," said Bacchus. "There is no sunshine here, nor any sound of the wind in the vine leaves."

Midas looked at the god in amazement.

"You talk like my daughter, Marigold," said he. "True, there is no sunshine here, but look! See the golden lights on these bowls, and the red glow on the jewels!"

"Have you seen the colors of grapes when the sun shines through them, purple and red and amber?" asked Bacchus.

"No," said Midas, "I like grapes only when they are brought to me on a golden platter. There is nothing in the world so lovely as gold. I wish that everything I touch might be changed into that beautiful metal. Then I should be happy."

"You shall have your wish," said Bacchus, hurrying away out of the gloomy room to his vineyards on the sunny hills.

"I shall have my wish!" whispered Midas delightedly. "Can he really mean it?"

Just then the palace servants struck the big gong and called the King to dinner.

Midas locked the door of his treasury and walked toward the room where his dinner awaited him. He glanced down at the great key in his hand. It was gold! His sleeve, too, gleamed a dull yellow and felt stiff to his touch. His girdle was changed into the same metal. His sandals, everything he wore, was shining gold.

He touched a marble column as he passed, and it turned yellow. The curtains which he brushed in passing grew rigid and gleaming.

Marigold came dancing in from the woods, her hands full of white anemones. She sat down in her tall chair beside the King's.

"Why, Father," she said, "when did you buy that funny stiff robe? And your yellow sandals, where did you get them?"

Midas smiled delightedly as he sat down. "They are solid gold, my dear! The gods have given me the Golden Touch. You may have anything in the world that you wish."

"Look at your chair, Father!" cried Marigold.

"No doubt it also is gold," smiled Midas, turning to see. "It seems more comfortable than ever. I shall have every chair in the palace made over."

He took his white napkin in his hand and shook it out. It was wonderful to see the golden color spread over the snowy linen, almost as if a yellow flame ran up the folds.

Smiling more than ever, he reached for his spoon. "We shall have all the golden dishes we like," he said.

Then he raised a spoonful of the savory soup to his mouth. He tasted it, and it was very good. But oh, horrible! When he tried to swallow it the taste vanished and there was nothing in his mouth but a hard lump. He choked and sputtered and coughed.

He looked at his plate in surprise.

"Can there be a stone in my soup?" he wondered. Midas tried another spoonful, but the same thing happened. He broke a piece of white bread, and it turned to gold as he raised it to his lips. He touched an apple and a pear. They became hard and glittering.

"Oh!" shouted the king, "I do not want my food to become gold. Everything else, O great god Bacchus, but not my food!"

Bacchus did not hear. He was far away in his vineyards listening to Pan's music. Marigold climbed down from her tall chair, and ran to the King.

"O dear Father," she said, "what has happened?"

She put her arms around his neck and her cheek to his. At the same moment her skin grew dark and yellow. The pink and white of her cheek vanished. Only her hair remained its own color, for her curls had always been like spun gold.

Midas put his hand on her to caress her, then drew away in terror. For his little daughter was now cold and hard, a golden statue.

"O Bacchus, O great Bacchus!" cried Midas, leaping to his feet, "take away this dreadful gift. My daughter has

"O great Bacchus," cried Midas, "take away this dreadful gift"

become a golden image. Everything I touch grows hard and cold. Give me back my little girl, or let me die!"

Bacchus heard at last, and came down from the hilltop and entered the palace.

"Well, Midas," he asked, "do you still care so much for gold?"

"No, no!" said the King. "Take away the Golden Touch and give me my Marigold."

Bacchus smiled wisely at the King.

"Perhaps now you will like the sunshine as much as gold, said the god, "and the glowing lights in grapes better than the glitter of stones. Perhaps now you will leave your treasure room sometimes and walk in the woods with Marigold."

"I will, I will!" promised Midas. "Only let her live again!"

"Then go to the river and wash," said Bacchus.

Midas ran as fast as he could out of the room and down the marble steps, which turned to gold as he passed. In the garden, the rose bushes which he brushed lost their green color and became tawny yellow. The gravel path changed, and the grass where he walked showed his footprints in yellow tracks.

Down the river bank Midas stumbled, and splashed into the water. His garments became soft and white. His girdle and sandals were of leather once more. But the river sands where he washed became golden, and remained so forever.

He ran back to the palace and took the golden figure
of little Marigold in his arms. At first she felt hard
and cold to his touch, but in a moment Marigold's

Midas splashed into the river

arms moved, her color returned, and she grew soft
and warm.

"O Father," she said, "I had a strange dream.
I dreamed that I could not speak, or move, or —"

"Never mind, my sweetheart," said the King, "that is all over."

"And I dreamed that your robe was made of gold—"

"But see, it is soft white linen now," said Midas. "Let us eat."

The servants brought more hot food, and Midas and his daughter finished their dinner. Never had soup tasted so good to him, nor fruit so juicy. His napkin seemed more beautiful in its snowy whiteness than any golden fabric he had ever seen.

When they rose from the table, Marigold showed him the white anemones.

"There are whole banks of them in the woods," she said. "And when the sun shines on them, and the wind blows, they look just like little dancing nymphs with yellow hair and white tunics. Won't you come with me and see them?"

"Indeed, yes," said Midas.

He put his hand in Marigold's and walked with her to the woods. There he found more happiness than he had ever known in his treasure room, and learned to love the white buds of flowers more than the largest pearls in his coffers.

PERSEUS AND ANDROMEDA

A fisherman was tending his nets one morning on the coast of Seriphus when he noticed something floating far out on the water. He rowed out and found a great wooden chest, which he towed to shore. When the fisherman pried up the heavy cover, he found inside the chest a beautiful princess with a little baby clasped in her arms.

A fisherman was tending his nets on the coast of Seriphus

The fisherman found inside the chest a beautiful princess with a little baby clasped in her arms

She had been shut in the chest for so many hours, floating over the sea, that she could not stand for weakness. So the fisherman lifted both baby and mother in his arms and carried them to the King.

Everyone in the palace was greatly surprised to see the strange princess and her baby. King Polydectes ordered food and wine for the mother, and the women of the palace bathed the baby and clothed him in fresh linen.

When the princess had eaten and felt refreshed, she told the King that her name was Danae and that her baby was Perseus, the little son of Jupiter. She told him that her father, King Acrisius of Argos, had shut them in the chest and set them afloat on the sea because he had heard from an oracle that some day the baby Perseus would grow up and cause his death.

Polydectes was delighted to have Danae stay in the palace, and for a long time he took care of her and her little son. But as Perseus grew up, Polydectes cared less for him, and finally began to wish that Perseus would go away.

So Polydectes sent him on a dangerous journey, to kill the gorgon Medusa, whose cavern was far away in the wilderness. Medusa's head was so terrible to see that no one could look at her without being turned into stone from sheer horror.

Perseus was glad to be sent on this adventure. He armed himself well and set out bravely toward the wilderness where Medusa dwelt.

Minerva, the goddess who watches over heroes, saw him depart, and feared that he could not succeed without the help of the gods. Perseus wore a sword and carried a shield and his sandals were light and strong, but Minerva knew that he would need weapons and armor more powerful than mortal sword or shield, and sandals swifter than his leathern ones.

Therefore she called upon Mercury, who brought his winged sandals of silver. Pluto, god of Erebus, lent his plumed helmet, which would make the wearer invisible.

Mercury brought his winged sandals, Pluto lent his plumed helmet,
and Minerva herself gave her shield

Minerva, herself, gave her shield, which nothing could pierce or shatter.

When Perseus strapped the winged sandals on his feet he felt himself rise with a strange lightness. When the helmet touched his head, he became invisible. With the strong and beautiful shield in his hand he set out, as swiftly as Mercury himself, flying through the air over tree tops and temples, toward the cavern of the Graeae.

He knew that these three aged sisters, the Graeae, were exceedingly wise, as wise as they were old, and that if they wished they could tell him where to find Medusa.

Medusa's head was terrible to see

As he drew near their cavern, he could hear them singing a mournful song, and, as he peered into the gloomy depths, he saw them rocking back and forth as they sang. They were bent and wrinkled and blind, except for one movable eye which they shared among them. They passed it back and forth as each took her turn at seeing. Their long white hair hung wild and loose on their shoulders.

As Perseus watched, one of them plucked the eye from her forehead and passed it to the sister next to her. For a moment she groped, reaching out for her sister's hand. Instantly, when all the Graeae were in darkness, Perseus sprang into the cavern and snatched the eye as it passed between their fingers.

For a moment there was terrible confusion, for each sister thought one of the others was hiding it. Then Perseus spoke to them and they knew that a stranger had stolen their eye. They stumbled around the cavern, blindly holding out their hands to find him, wailing and pleading all the time.

Perseus was sorry for them, but he did not intend to return their eye until they told him where to find the Gorgon. The Graeae were willing to do anything to have their eye again, and so they agreed to give Perseus all the help they could. They told him exactly in which direction he must go, and just how to find the cavern of Medusa.

Perseus returned their eye and thanked them. Then, swiftly, he flew to the home of Medusa.

Perseus found the entrance to her cave exactly where the Graeae had told him. On every side stood figures of stone, their faces turned toward the cavern. They wore such an expression of terror that Perseus was careful to keep his face turned away, lest he should see Medusa.

From inside the cave he could hear strange noises, as of some one walking about and complaining. He heard the whispering sound made by the hissing of the serpents which formed Medusa's hair.

Hiding himself behind one of the stone images he waited until nightfall, then stole up quietly and found the spot where Medusa slept. Although he kept his head turned aside, he could see her reflection in the brightness of his shield.

Bending over, Perseus cut off the Gorgon's head, and carrying it with him hurried to the entrance of the cave. He rose into the air, and flew over the sea and over Africa. As he passed, some drops of the Gorgon's blood fell on the sands of the African desert and immediately changed into poisonous serpents.

At length Perseus came to the realm of a king named Atlas. When he asked for food and rest, Atlas refused him and drove him from the palace doors.

Perseus uncovered the head of Medusa and raised it in front of Atlas. As soon as the King beheld it, he was turned to stone. As Perseus watched, Atlas grew larger and larger. His hips formed the slopes of a mighty mountain; his hair and beard became forests, and thrusting his head high among the stars, he was forced to receive the weight of the sky on his shoulders. Forever after he was doomed to bear that burden.

Perseus flew on until he came to the land of Ethiopia. Here he noticed a group of people on the shore, wringing their hands and weeping. Chained to a nearby rock he saw a maiden who kept her face turned toward the sea. She seemed to be expecting something to approach from across the water.

Perseus floated down and, as he came near her, he found that she was the loveliest maiden he had ever beheld. He took off his invisible helmet and spoke to her thus:

"O Virgin, undeserving of those chains, tell me, I beseech you, your name and the name of your country, and why you are thus bound."

Replying, the maiden told Perseus that she was Andromeda, Princess of Ethiopia. She was bound to the rock to await the coming of a sea-dragon which would devour her because the gods of the sea were angry with her mother.

Being beautiful and proud of her charms, the Queen of Ethiopia had boasted that she was lovelier than the sea nymphs. Neptune's daughters were angry at this boast, and as a punishment they sent a dreadful sea-dragon to carry off the fairest youths and maidens that lived in the land.

At last the King and Queen were warned by the gods that they must chain their own daughter to a rock so that the dragon might be given the loveliest maiden in all the kingdom. Then, said the oracle, the dragon would be satisfied and would return to the depths of the sea from which he had come.

Even as Andromeda was telling these things to Perseus they heard a roaring sound that came from the sea. As they looked up a huge green monster swam swiftly

As the dragon came near, Perseus darted downward like an eagle

across the water, throwing great fountains of spray toward the heavens.

Perseus sprang into the air. As the dragon came near, he darted downward like an eagle and buried his sword in the serpent's shoulder. Such a fight followed that Andromeda covered her eyes in terror.

The monster lashed his tail to the right and to the left, and in his fury split great rocks. Again and again Perseus rose into the air and swooped down upon him, wounding him until at last he lay still, partly in the water and partly on shore, his head and body stretched on the rocks and the sand, his tail floating far out on the sea.

Perseus unbound the Princess, and the King and Queen gave a great banquet in his honor. Then they allowed him to marry Andromeda and carry her back to his own land.

Perseus returned the helmet to Pluto, the shield to Minerva, and the winged sandals to Mercury, and forever after lived happily with Andromeda.

The oracle which declared that Perseus would cause the death of King Acrisius spoke truly. For one day, after Perseus had returned to his own land, he was playing with the discus and threw it in a course too curved. With a flash of light like that of a swinging sword, the sharp discus flew beyond the limits of the field and struck the King a mortal blow. Thus the words of the ancient oracle came true.

PYGMALION AND GALATEA

Beautiful girls came walking by Pygmalion's window

Pygmalion was a sculptor who could think of nothing but his chisels and the marble and ivory with which he loved to work. Beautiful Greek girls came walking by his window, and peeped in at the door to watch him, but he never raised his head or paid the least attention to them.

Pygmalion spent all his time admiring and adoring the figure he had made

One day Pygmalion chose the largest, most perfect piece of ivory in the kingdom. When the laborers had brought it to his home, he took his keenest tools and began to carve the ivory with delicate care.

"There is no maiden living," said Pygmalion, "so beautiful as this statue that I shall make."

For weeks he worked, stopping only to eat, and at night to throw himself on the floor beside the statue to rest.

Day by day the figure grew more lovely. At last it seemed so perfect that nothing could be done to make it more wonderful. Still Pygmalion worked, smoothing and carving the ivory until it was indeed more beautiful than any Greek maiden in the land.

When the statue was finished, Pygmalion clothed it in soft garments and hung jewels around the ivory neck. He spent all his time admiring and adoring the figure he had made. He named it "Galatea," which means "Sleeping Love."

Just at this time there was in Pygmalion's city a festival in honor of Venus, the goddess of beauty and of love. Pygmalion went to her temple. He offered gifts at her altar, and prayed that she would give him for his bride a living maiden exactly like his beautiful ivory statue.

Venus had been standing unseen beside her altar. When she heard Pygmalion's prayer, she left her temple and went to the sculptor's home to see the figure of which he was so fond.

The goddess was delighted with the loveliness of Pygmalion's statue. She thought it looked much like herself. This pleased her so that she touched the cold ivory and bade it live.

She laid her fingers on the waving hair and it became soft and lustrous. The cheeks grew pink, the eyes blue, and the lips like coral.

When Pygmalion returned and entered his home, the statue no longer stood in its usual corner. Instead, a beautiful maiden with golden hair and skin like ivory flushed with the color of sunrise walked toward him.

Pygmalion watched in amazement. When he saw that his statue lived and moved, he threw himself on the floor and clasped her feet. They were warm and rosy.

Galatea looked down at him, smiling and touching his hair with her slender fingers.

Pygmalion did not forget to offer thanks to the goddess. He built an altar to Venus of ivory and gold and carved it with all manner of blossoms and birds.

Every day as long as Pygmalion and Galatea lived, they offered gifts at the altar, and Venus in return blessed them with happiness and love.

ROMULUS AND REMUS

Romulus and Remus were twin babies. Their mother died when they were very tiny. No one else loved them enough to care for them, so they were placed in a watertight basket and sent floating down the river Tiber.

Romulus and Remus reminded the wolf of her own babies

The winds took care not to ripple the surface of the water, lest the basket tip. The sun shone on the babies and warmed them as they drifted slowly down the river. It was very much like being rocked in a mother's warm arms.

Although the Tiber could carry them gently on his breast, and the winds could watch over them, and the sun could keep them warm, there was one thing that still troubled the babies. They were hungry and had no milk.

Then the river Tiber called all the little streams which emptied their water into his. They poured into the Tiber until he overflowed his banks and the basket was carried high on the sand. Then the water drew back and left the babies on dry land.

A mother wolf came prowling beside the river, looking for food. When she saw the basket she trotted over. Romulus and Remus were crying and putting their fists in their mouths. Somehow they reminded the wolf of her own babies, although her own cubs were covered with fur and could stand on their feet.

She licked the babies with her tongue, but never once thought of eating them. She rolled them out of the basket with her paw, and pushed them ever so gently over the sand and grass to her cave.

Dragging them inside, she put them in the nest where her little wolves were sleeping. They wakened as she stretched herself beside them, and crowded around her to get their milk. Romulus and Remus drank too, and went to sleep cuddled up close to their strange new mother.

For many weeks they lived in the cave and played with the little wolves, rolling over and over and wrestling with them. They grew strong and could walk long before other babies.

One day they crept to the opening of the cave and saw the blue sky and the sunshine. After that the mother wolf had a hard time keeping them inside. One day when she was away a shepherd came by and saw the two babies playing on the grass. He carried them home to his wife, who brought them up as her own children.

The twins often ran back to the cave

She taught them to drink from cups, and made them tunics to wear. They grew to love the shepherd and his wife, but they never forgot their wolf mother, and often ran back to the cave to see her and romp in the sunshine with her cubs.

They loved to play beside the river, and wade and swim in the warm water, or dig in the sand.

"When I am grown," said Romulus, "I shall build a house beside the Tiber"

"When I am grown," said Romulus, "I shall build a house with wide porches and tall columns of marble beside the Tiber."

Little Remus did not live to grow up. But years after, Romulus built his house on the banks of the Tiber near the cave where the mother wolf had nursed him.

He had many friends who came and built their houses near by. In time a beautiful city grew up, and Romulus was so strong and wise that the people made him their ruler. That was the beginning of the great city of Rome, which still stands and grows beside the River Tiber.

INDEX OF CHARACTERS

Thousands of years ago, the ancient Greeks worshipped many gods and goddesses and told wondrous tales about them. Centuries later, these gods were still being worshipped and their legends were still being told by the Romans. Many of the names changed, but their stories remained much the same. Here is an alphabetical list of the gods, heroes, monsters, and others appearing in this collection of Myths and Enchantment Tales. Greek names are mainly used, but a few — especially those of the gods — are Roman. The name listed first is the name used in this book. Roman names appear in **bold type**; the others are Greek. The page numbers following each description show where the character may be found in the book. *Italicized* page numbers indicate an illustration.

Acrisius: mortal; King of Argos; father of Danae, 142, 149

Admetus: mortal; good and wise King of Thessaly, 48, *48*

Amphitryon: mortal; earthly father of Hercules; 19–21

Anaxarete: mortal; noblewoman turned to stone for refusing to love, 70–72

Andromeda: mortal; Princess of Ethiopia; wife of Perseus, 146–149, *148*

Apollo, Apollo or Phoebus Apollo: son of Jupiter; god of the sun and the arts, 2, 10, 15, *26*, 27–33, *32*, 66, 78–83, *80*, 97, 113, 117–122, *118*

Arcas: mortal; son of Callisto, 126–130, *127*, *128*, *129*

Aristaeus: mortal; son of water-nymph, Cyrene; keeper of the bees, 110

Atalanta: mortal; raised by a bear; could run faster than any other mortal, 73–77, *76*

Atlas: Titan; was turned into stone and made to carry heavens on his shoulders, 22–24, 146

Augeas: mortal; king of the Epeians, 22

Bacchus, Dionysus: god of wine and joy, 131–137, *136*

Bellerophon: mortal; Prince of Corinth and son of Glaucus; rode the winged horse, Pegasus, 34–42, *35*, *38*, *40*

Boreas: the north wind, 73

Callisto: woodland nymph living in Arcady; changed to a bear by Juno, 126–130

Castor: mortal; son of Jupiter and mortal Leda; twin brother of Pollux, 48, *48*

Celeus: mortal; his family comforts Ceres upon the loss of her daughter, Prosperpina, to Pluto, 89–91, *90*

centaurs: half man, half horse; living in the mountains of Thessaly, 44, 109, 111

Cereberus: monster; three-headed dog guarding the gates of the underworld, 85, 93, 104–106, 110–112

Ceres, Demeter: sister of Jupiter; goddess of the harvest, 87–95, *89*, 101–102

Chaemera: dragon that terrorizes the kingdom of Lycia, 35–41, *40*

Charon: god dwelling in the underworld; boatman across the river Styx, 94, 104–105, *105*, 110–116

Chiron: centaur; master of school for Greek princes, 44, 48

Circe: mortal; enchantress dwelling on the island of Eaea, 55–61, *58*, *61*

Clymene: mortal; mother of Phaeton, *117*, 119

Cupid, Eros: son of Venus; god of love, 12, *14*, 78–81, *79*, *80*, 87, 96–108, *97*, *100*

Cybele, Rhea: mother of Jupiter, 77

Daedalus: mortal; inventor imprisoned with

son, Icarus, by King Minos on the island of Crete, 63–66

Danae: mortal; mother of Perseus, 140–142, *141*

Daphne: nymph loved by Apollo, 81–83, *82, 83*

Danaus, daughters of: spirits inhabiting the underworld, 114

Diana, Artemis: daughter of Jupiter and the mortal Latona; goddess of the moon, the hunt, and young maidens, 27–33, *32*

dryads: wood nymphs, 109–111

Eetes (or Aeetes): mortal; King of Colchis, father of Medea, 49–53

Epimetheus: Titan; Prometheus' brother; prepared Earth for the coming of man, 8, 9–16

Eurolochus: mortal; member of Ulysses' crew, 55–61

Eurydice: mortal; wife of Orpheus, 109–116, *113, 115*

fauns: half man, half goat; like satyrs, neither god nor human, 68, 109

Furies, Erinyes: avenging goddesses dwelling in the underworld, 114

Galatea: statue-turned-mortal; sculpted and loved by Pygmalion, 151–153, *152*

Glaucus: mortal; King of Corinth, 34

Graeae: monsters; three wise, aged sisters with but one shared eye, 144–145

Harpies: monsters; part woman, part bird, 49

Hebe, **Juventas:** daughter of Jupiter; cupbearer to the gods; goddess of youth, 107, *107*

Helios: second god to drive the chariot of the sun after his father, Hyperion, 31, *32*

Helle: mortal; Phrixus' sister; falls from golden-fleeced ram's back at place called Hellespont, 45–46, *47*

Hercules, Herakles: divine hero; son of Jupiter; becomes an immortal after many wondrous deeds, 19–25, *19, 20, 24*

Hesperides: personification of twilight; daughters of Hesperus; keepers of garden where the golden apples grow, 22, *23*

Hesperus: personification of the evening star; father of the Hesperides, 22

Hippomenes: mortal; races Atalanta and wins with the help of Venus, 73–77, *74, 76*

Hydra: monster; nine-headed water serpent slain by Hercules, 21

Hyperboreans: mortals; people living beyond the north wind in a place of perpetual spring and summer, 30–31

Hyperion: first god to drive the chariot of the sun, 31

Icarus: mortal; son of Daedalus; imprisoned by King Minos on the island of Crete, *62,* 63–66, *64*

Iobates: mortal; King of Lycia; challenges Prince Bellerophon to kill the Chaemera, 35–36, 41

Iphis: mortal; kills himself for love of Anaxarete, 70

Jason: mortal; Prince of Iolcus in Thessaly; seeks the Golden Fleece, 43–54, *48, 51*

Juno, Hera: wife and sister of Jupiter; queen of the gods and ruler of heaven and earth, 12, 19, 22, 27–28, 44–54, 126–130, *130*

Jupiter, Zeus: king of the gods; ruler of heaven and earth; dwells on Mount Olympus, 10–14, 19, 22, 23–25, 27, 30–33, 41, 77, 86, 92–94, 106–108, 125, 126–130, *129,* 142

Latona, Leto: mortal; mother of Apollo and Diana, 27–30, *28, 29*

Linus: mortal; Hercules' music teacher, 21

Mars, Ares: son of Jupiter; god of war, 50

Medea: mortal; Princess of Colchis; daughter of Eetes; enchantress, 50–54

Medusa: monster; has poisonous snakes for hair; turns foes to stone at the sight of her, 142–146, *144*

Mercury, Hermes: son of Jupiter; messenger of the gods, 12–13, *13,* 15, 45, 59, 73, 92–95, *93,* 107, 142–144, *143,* 149

Midas: mortal; king who loves gold above all else, 131–139, *136, 138*

Minerva, Athena: daughter of Jupiter; goddess of wisdom and justice, 12, 34, *36,* 37, 41, 42, 142–143, *143,* 149

Minos: son of Jupiter and mortal Europa; King of Crete; judge of the dead, 63

Nephele: true mother of Phrixus and Helle, 45

Neptune, Poseidon: god and ruler of the oceans, 130, 147 nymphs: beings resembling maidens; neither god nor human; dwelling in nature, 34, 67–68, 81, 87–92, 89, 109–111, 126–127, 147

Orpheus: mortal; son of musical muse, Calliope; tries to rescue his wife, Eurydice, from the underworld, 48, 48, 109–116, 111, 112, 115

Pan: god of flocks and shepherds; piper with goat's legs, 68, 69, 109

Pandora: Titan; a gift from the gods as a companion for Epimetheus, 12–18, 17

Pegasus: Minerva's winged horse; ridden by Bellerophon, 34–42, 38, 40

Pelias: mortal; brother of the King of Iolcus, 43–54

Peneus: god of the river Peneus; father of Daphne, 81–82

Perseus: mortal; son of Jupiter and the mortal Danae; slays Medusa and rescues Andromeda from a sea-dragon, 23, 140–149, 141, 148

Phaeton: mortal; son of Apollo and mortal Clymene, 117–125, 117, 118, 121, 123, 124

Phrixus: mortal; escapes from harm on back of golden-fleeced ram, 45–46, 47

Pluto, Hades: god of the underworld, 84, 85–95, 86, 104, 112–116, 142, 143, 149

Pollux: mortal; son of Jupiter and mortal Leda; twin brother of Castor, 48, 48

Polydectes: mortal; king; protector of Danae and young Perseus, 141–142

Polyidus: mortal; oldest and wisest man in the kingdom of Lycia, 37

Pomona: nymph; caretaker of fruit-bearing trees of the orchard, 67–72, 67, 71, 72

Proetus: mortal; son-in-law of Iobates, the King of Lycia, 34, 35

Prometheus: Titan; was punished by gods for bringing fire to man, 9–11, 11, 12, 25

Prosperpina, Persephone: daughter of Ceres; Pluto's wife and goddess of the underworld, 84, 87–95, 95, 104–106, 113–116

Psyche: mortal; princess who falls in love with Cupid and is made an Immortal, 96–108, 97, 99, 103, 105, 108

Pygmalion: mortal; creator of Galatea, the statue Venus brings to life for him to love, 150–153, 152

Python: monster; dragon or serpent, 78, 81

Remus: mortal; raised by wolves; twin brother of Romulus, 154–157, 154, 156, 157

Romulus: mortal; raised by wolves; twin brother of Remus; founder of Rome, 154–157, 154, 156, 157

satyrs: half man, half goat; like fauns, neither god nor human, 68, 109

Silenus: forest god; companion of Bacchus, 132

Tantalus: spirit inhabiting the underworld, 114

Thea (or Theia): keeper of the moon before Diana, 32

Theseus: mortal; King of Athens; performed many great deeds, 48, 48

Ulysses, Odysseus: mortal; King of Ithaca and Greek leader in the Trojan War; 55–63, 55, 61

Venus, Aphrodite: daughter of Jupiter; goddess of love and beauty, 12–15, 14, 75, 77, 78–81, 96–108, 103, 151–153

Vertumnus: god of the changing seasons, 68–72, 72

Vulcan, Hephaestus: son of Jupiter; god of fire and keeper of the forge, 11, 13–14, 31, 79

Zephyr: the west wind, 73, 98–101, 99